THE WARD'S BRIDE

BORDER SERIES PREQUEL

CECELIA MECCA

ALTIORA
PRESS

To mom, my inspiration for strong heroines

CHAPTER 1

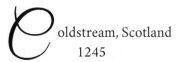 oldstream, Scotland
1245

"Richard, this is madness."

Sir Adam Dayne looked back across the river into England, where men were wading through the ford as he and Richard had done moments before.

"It will never work," Richard agreed.

As they approached the waiting Scotsmen, Adam's hand itched to grab the hilt of his sword. Their directive was clear—there would be no fighting—but when he looked into the faces of their enemies, Adam was convinced it would be near impossible to avoid bloodshed.

The crisp autumn air reminded him of another day nearly a year ago when he, Richard, and Richard's father, the second earl of Kenshire, had come to this same spot. They'd crossed the River Tweed to meet with the Scottish lord warden of the Eastern Marches to negotiate the terms of this first "Day of Truce." The long-time enemies would meet in peace to hold trials for accused border reivers from both sides. The wardens believed it was the first step in finally ending the violence that had plagued the border between England and Scotland.

It had been decided the English would be the ones to cross the river. The Scots had argued that they were always forced to appeal for peace following a cessation of war and that it was therefore their right for the truce to be held in Scotland. Acting as the host, however, meant they would provide sustenance for both sides.

Adam had never thought this day would come to pass, yet here they were. He and Richard stopped at the agreed-upon spot and awaited a signal from Richard's father and the Scottish warden. At a glance, it was clear their Scottish counterparts were as skeptical as they were about the success of this day. Amidst tents that dotted the open fields before him, men in various dress glared at them. Some were openly prepared for battle, the chainmail of the nobles in stark contrast to the understated tunics of the other soldiers. But one thing was evident of all. These men were not as invested in peace as their leader.

"If you weren't so large, Adam, I could see what was happening." Richard peered around his shoulder. "My father looks none too pleased."

"I don't see a man present who looks pleased to be here," Adam responded. "I have a bad feeling."

Richard looked behind them. "A bad feeling about bringing together two hundred Englishmen and Scotsmen, accused criminals, and only my father, the Maxwell, and a couple of bailiffs to keep the peace? You're not just a celebrated knight, Sir Adam, but a true visionary."

One fully armored soldier without a crest to identify him glared at them with an expression that could only mean one thing. He would like nothing more than to use the war hammer hanging at his side to dispense with either Adam or Richard. Or mayhap both. Luckily, he was far enough away not to overhear their conversation.

Adam smiled at his friend under his nasal helm. "I don't think our counterparts appreciate your humor."

"If you think I—"

"Look!" Adam interrupted his friend to point at the Marcher wardens. Both had raised their hands in the air, eliciting shouts from the men standing on either side of them. This was the signal that all was to go as planned.

Richard's father lowered his hand and turned to address the men.

"As lord warden of the Eastern March, it is my duty to remind all present to act with honor," he shouted. "Our intention is for this first Day of Truce to be the start of a better relationship between our peoples. I will have your assent that you will not offend by word, deed, or countenance this day."

Adam and Richard raised their fists into the air and the other Englishmen followed suit.

Sir John Maxwell, Scottish warden of the Eastern March, repeated the phrase to his men, who raised their fists in the air as a sign of acceptance.

"I don't believe that man understands the meaning of offense by countenance," said Richard in an undertone.

Adam held back a smile.

Finally, both the English and Scottish bailiffs stepped forward. Now that the official proceedings had begun, men from both sides visibly relaxed.

For the remainder of the morning, Adam and Richard stayed close to Lord Kenshire. And while tensions remained high, Adam started to wonder if this brokered peace might actually work. He left Richard in search of sustenance. Removing his helm and entering the tent that had been raised by the Scotsmen, he watched as enemies spoke to each other as cordially as could be expected. He even briefly conversed with a clan chief, who admitted he never thought this day would come to pass.

After claiming a hunk of bread, he made his way back into the open field. Shouts and a gathering crowd nearby drew his attention. Although weapons had been banned, no one had heeded that particular mandate, and Adam lowered his hand to the hilt of his sword as he made his approach. He pushed his way through the increasingly angry crowd and stopped short at the sight before him.

Richard lay flat on the ground. An Englishman Adam didn't know reached out his hand and Richard grabbed it. Nearby, two Scotsmen held back one of their own men—the main source of the shouting—but he continued to spew obscenities.

"Richard—" Adam pushed his way next to him, "—are you unhurt?"

"Aye, thanks to him." Richard nodded to the man who'd helped him up. He was likely their age, eight and twenty, and his crest was unfamiliar.

"What the devil happened?" Adam immediately recognized the voice: Richard's father.

The crowd parted for Lord Kenshire and Lord Maxwell. The men had cause to be concerned. Their carefully brokered Day of Truce was on the verge of becoming a battlefield.

"Silence!" Lord Kenshire had been appointed the English warden for a reason. His shout was loud and authoritative enough to momentarily quite the crowd.

"English scum. May the devil take your soul!" said the Scot who was being held.

Adam recognized him as the same man who'd glared at him and Richard that morning.

"What's the meaning of this?" Lord Maxwell asked, none too gently.

"Your man tried to stab me from behind," Richard explained. He then pointed to the English knight. "This man, who I know not, saw everything." He lowered his voice, but Adam was close enough to hear him clearly. "He saved my life."

Everyone began talking at once. The hope drained out of Adam. This would destroy any gains they'd made this day.

"Is there another man to verify this story?" asked the formidable Scottish lord.

His kinsman, who still restrained the accused, spoke up. "Aye, my lord. He did indeed attempt to stab the Englishman in the back." The man spat on the ground. It seemed his sense of honor was stronger than his hatred of the English. Adam nodded in agreement. He would have done the same. To his mind, any man who failed to face another when he ended his life deserved to die.

It would seem Lord Maxwell agreed, for he immediately replied, "Take him away. This day will be his last."

Although the disgraced man was led away by his own kinsman, the crowd was anything but appeased.

"What the hell happened, Richard?" Adam asked.

While the wardens conferred with each other, the men shifted and blustered, uneasy now that the rules had been broken.

"It was as I said," Richard replied. "If it weren't for...what's your name, my good man?"

Richard's savior lifted his chin. His jet-black hair and dark eyes lent him a distinctly ominous look.

"Sir Hugh Waryn, at your service."

Richard waved his hand dismissively. "There'll be no formalities between us. You just saved my life. I'm forever in your debt." Richard bowed and then clasped the man's arm. "My brother, Adam, and I are pleased to make your acquaintance."

Sir Hugh drew his eyebrows and Adam clarified. "Brother by kinship, not by blood."

"I see. Well, it seems we—"

"Sir Richard. Sir Adam. Come." Lord Kenshire summoned them to his side. Conversation with Sir Hugh would have to wait.

"You're unhurt, my son?"

"Aye, Father."

Lord Kenshire turned to Adam. "The attempted murder of my

son by a wayward member of Lord Maxwell's clan threatens to undo everything we've set out to accomplish."

One look around confirmed his words. This unrest could easily shift into battle, but what did his foster father want from him?

"Aye, my lord."

"Lord Maxwell and I have come to an agreement. A way to ensure peace is kept on this important day."

The glance the wardens exchanged was Adam's first indication he would not like what the earl was about to say.

"This Day of Truce is needed to bring justice to those who deserve it. If unsuccessful, the future of the border, on both sides, is in jeopardy."

The crowd, raucous and on edge moments before, had grown remarkably quiet. It seemed he wasn't the only one anxious to hear what the wardens had planned.

"I understand, my lord." And he did. Adam had been raised by Spencer Caiser since he was a lad of one and ten. He knew the man well and could ascertain his moods. This was as serious as he'd ever seen him.

"Lord Maxwell has pledged his eldest daughter's hand in marriage in good faith to recompense for this unfortunate incident."

All eyes turned to him. Finally, the earl's purpose was clear. Others likely wondered why Lord Kenshire's own son had not been brokered for peace. But that was not possible. Sir Richard was already betrothed.

"Lord Maxwell knows you are as a son to me. He understands you are the most skilled knight in my service. And now I bequeath to you Lordship of Langford Castle and its demesne. I will have your oath of fealty this day."

He didn't know what to say. Lordship? Langford Castle? He knew Spencer thought highly of him, he'd spent his life ensuring it was so, but he had never expected this.

Adam looked at Richard, who smiled broadly. One would never guess the man's life had been threatened a moment ago. Had he known this was coming? Langford should have been part of Richard's inheritance by right, but he looked neither surprised nor displeased.

Was this done only to appease Lord Maxwell? Because he knew what was coming next.

"As such, he agreed that you will be a more than suitable husband for his daughter, Lady Cora."

The earl watched him closely. Adam knew nothing of the girl and had certainly never imagined a Scottish wife. But there was only one possible answer.

He nodded his head to Spencer and bowed to Lord Maxwell. "I would be honored, my lord, to take your daughter as my wife."

CHAPTER 2

angford Castle, Southern England

Flanked by her father on one side and the captain of the guard on her other, Cora felt utterly and truly trapped. As they ascended to the top of a rise, she pulled her fur-lined cloak more firmly about her shoulders. While the days were still somewhat warm, the air turned cool well before nightfall. Winter would be upon them soon, and unless she succeeded in her efforts to disrupt this arranged marriage, she'd spend it in England.

She looked down upon her future home. She'd seen this type of structure before. Unlike her own home, Langford's keep rose above all the other buildings around it. Even from this distance, she could see guards on the wall-walk that surrounded the keep. The bailey hosted an impressive number of buildings, all enclosed by a palisade.

"Well-fortified," her father said.

Of course that would be his primary concern. The man was every inch a soldier. He seemed to forget that an Englishman she didn't know waited below them to take her as a wife.

"'Tis English," she said flatly.

8

His answer was a hard look. They'd had this discussion a number of times after his grand announcement three weeks earlier: she did not want to be a pawn in the border wars; he insisted he'd had no choice.

He urged his mount forward, and their small party closed the distance to her future home. At least, her temporary future home.

While they waited for the drawbridge to lower, her father continued his appeal. If Cora had not been so miserable, she might have appreciated his tenacity.

"I didn't expect it to be so green this far south. Look, Cora." He pointed to the rolling hills that surrounded them. "We could be in Scotland."

She rolled her eyes. While she should be grateful her father cared enough to try and soften her to her banishment to England, Cora had a hard time summoning anything but resentment and anger.

The drawbridge lowered, and a shudder ran through her. True, Langford was well-fortified, but it had obviously been sorely neglected in other areas. Weeds grew where flowers should have been planted. And though they'd met more and more people the farther south they'd traveled, it had struck Cora that none of them were on their way here. Admittedly, they'd skirted the nearest village, not wanting to draw attention, but it was not an auspicious sign.

"I'm told Langford's keep was recently rebuilt," Cora's father said as they rode across the bridge and into the courtyard.

She glanced up at the stone structure in the distance, towering high above the other buildings. Surely he could see, as she did, that this holding was in dire need of upkeep. "I'm sure it's the finest keep in all of England."

Her father clearly did not appreciate her tone, for he urged his mount forward. Cora was glad for it. She had no desire to speak to the man who had forsaken his daughter in favor of peace with their enemy.

Day of Truce.

How could her father want anything other than revenge on the men who stole and murdered her people? But that was her father. Although they never said as much to their lord, most members of Clan Maxwell wanted nothing to do with brokering peace along the border. They cared little for talk of border lines and justice.

As they rode closer to the castle, they passed many people. Englishmen and women. The sight of a woman pulling her son close, away from the galloping horses, made Cora think of her own mother. When would she see her again? She thought of the sealed parchment her mother had given her. Her mother never learned to write, so she must have had assistance composing it.

Even still, Cora refused to open it. She was sure it was nothing more than praise for doing her "duty." And her sister? Could she really convince this English lord to break their betrothal? Her father and his men expected to remain at Langford for a few weeks until the wedding. Surely that would be enough time for her to convince Sir Adam they were ill-suited.

They rode through the outer bailey into a second smaller courtyard with more activity. A miller and blacksmith shop, servants going about their business—all stopped what they were doing and stared as their party halted at the foot of the second drawbridge, where a small group awaited them. Cora reluctantly dismounted with the help of a young groom.

She hadn't expected Sir Adam to greet them, and it came as a relief that he clearly had not.

"Welcome." A stately older gentleman bowed to her father and then to her. "I am Charles, steward of Langford Castle. My lord regrets his absence this evening. A house in the village caught fire, which spread to neighboring establishments. We've received word the fire has finally been contained, but my lord is assessing the damages."

As the steward spoke, a small, curious crowd gathered. They undoubtedly knew the new lord was to wed a Scottish woman, and Cora imagined they were as anxious as she about the prospect.

"No apologies are necessary," her father replied.

The steward turned and said something to a nearby servant, who hurried away. Moments later, the second drawbridge lowered. The wooden planks creaked beneath their feet as they made their way to the rock stairs built into the man-made hill supporting the keep. When she arrived at the top, Cora took a deep breath before entering the foreboding building.

"This way," the steward pointed to a small set of stairs, which led to the first floor and the keep's great hall. Just as she'd suspected. It lacked a woman's touch. Stone walls uncovered... clean but unscented rushes...just enough candles to give light but none to highlight any decoration. Cora pulled her cloak tighter. Tapestries would help keep out the chill.

Servants stacked trestle tables, marking the end of the evening meal. They all stopped working to stare at the newcomers. Cora had known she would be an outsider here, but must every person they meet look upon them as if they'd never seen a Scot before? Had these English no manners to speak of? And they were supposed to be the barbarians.

A plump woman who appeared to be the same age as the steward hurried toward them. Her posture, erect for a woman with white-streaked hair in servant's garb, marked her as someone accustomed to giving orders. Cora guessed she was Langford's housekeeper.

Confirming her assessment, the steward introduced them: "Mistress Clare, may I present Lord Maxwell, his daughter Lady Cora, and members of Clan Maxwell. Clare is Langford's housekeeper."

The woman bowed deeply to them without the curious glances they'd received from the other servants. "Would ye prefer to dine in the hall or have a meal brought to yer room?"

Cora spoke up for the first time since their arrival. "I would like to retire, mistress, if you please." She turned to her father. "Good eve, if you'll excuse me, sire."

Without giving him a chance to answer, Cora turned and prepared to follow Clare. She had expected her father to stop her, but the steward's voice was the one that rang out behind her.

"I believe my lord would like to speak with you before you retire."

Does he sound worried?

She spun back around. His expression left no doubt that something was amiss. Though there were few windows, and it was darker inside than it had been out, the steward's face was lit by nearby candles. He looked pale even at a distance.

"Surely Sir Adam would deem sunrise a sufficient time to speak to me after our long journey."

Or mayhap the man was as rude as she imagined him to be.

Rather than answer her directly, the steward leaned toward her father. They conferred quietly and Cora resisted the urge to protest. If she were at home, in Scotland, such a blatant dismissal would not go unaddressed. But her "propensity to speak her mind," as her father so indelicately put it, would not be welcome in this instance—just as it had not been welcome these past weeks. She took a deep breath instead.

When a discomfited look surfaced on her father's face, Cora nearly broke her silence, but she managed to wait—somewhat impatiently—for him to explain.

"Go, my dear," he said instead. "I will speak with Sir Adam on your behalf. Master Charles, we will take our meal here if you'd be so kind."

The steward looked as if he wanted to say something, but he merely looked at the housekeeper and shook his head. *What could be happening?*

The housekeeper urged her toward the stairs.

"The lord and lady's...pardon...*yer* chamber is here," she said, pointing to private rooms at the end of the corridor. "But for tonight, I've had the adjoining bower prepared for you." She opened a large wooden door, and Cora stepped into the room that would serve as her temporary bedchamber. Until she could leave this place and return to Scotland, of course. Mayhap she should have waited up to speak to the Englishman this eve.

Nay, tomorrow would be soon enough to begin her campaign.

Where would her father and their men stay? As if reading her thoughts about sleeping arrangements, Clare turned down the covers on the fine-looking four-poster bed. "I'll have a pallet brought in, if it pleases you, for me to sleep here tonight."

Cora heard the question in her voice.

"My thanks, Mistress Clare. My own woman fell ill on the second day of our journey and returned home." Cora wished she could have done the same, although she certainly didn't need a chaperone. She didn't intend to go near the English lord, never mind conduct herself in a way that could be deemed inappropriate. Nevertheless, it would be rude to say so.

"My thanks for the fire, mistress." It radiated a welcoming warmth.

"Clare." The clearly capable woman was already scurrying around, lighting candles from the hearth fire and spreading them throughout the chamber. "'Tis my job, my lady."

Cora caught sight of streaks of grey under the servant's cap. "How long have you been at Langford?"

"I was born here and, by the grace of God, will die here too."

Cora sat on the edge of the bed and looked toward the door at the far end of the room. "And the new lord?"

Now why had she asked such a question? She cared not about him. It wasn't as if they were actually getting married.

Clare stopped in front of her and smiled. Wrinkles formed at the corners of her light green eyes, nearly the exact shade of Cora's own. But unlike her "devil's red hair" as her sister liked to say, Clare's looked as if it was once a shade of brown. Now there was more grey than not under her cap, so it was difficult to tell.

"We're pleased to have 'im," Clare said. "The old lord died without an heir. When the king granted Langford to the earl, we were all a mite worried. We'd been over two years, as ye can see, without anyone but Charles overseeing the place. It's lucky we weren't attacked."

Interesting, but Clare had not exactly recommended Sir Adam. Why? Was he cruel? What did he look like? She yawned.

Nay. She would not ask because she did not care. Her future would not be relegated to an ancient keep in Southern England. She belonged back home, in Scotland, with her family and clan.

After Clare helped her undress, Cora let herself recline on the bed for a moment. Sounds startled her awake some time later, mayhap the servant bringing a meal, but she slipped back into an exhausted slumber. The next morning she awoke to find sunlight streaming onto her cheek from the lone slit in the wall.

"'Tis a fine morning for a wedding! Up my dear, there's much to be done."

Cora stretched her arms, refreshed by her slumber, and her mood was not even dampened when she remembered the night before. A fine morning indeed for a...

She bolted off the bed.

"What did you say?"

Clare just cocked her head, giving her an odd look, before she returned to what she was doing—fussing over a dress. The emerald green one Cora had packed in her trunk. The one her mother had insisted she wear for her wedding to the Englishman. Though Cora's mother and sister had wished to be part of her escort, her father had insisted the journey would be "too dangerous" for them.

Her shoulders slumped as she remembered the hushed conversation between her father and the steward the previous evening. Sir Adam had wanted to speak to her. Her father had promised to do so on her behalf.

How could she have been so stupid? But she couldn't have

known this was afoot—the plan had been for them to marry toward the end of her clan's visit. What had happened to change things? Could her betrothed have divined her intentions?

Well, she wouldn't do it. There was no way she was getting married today.

The door opened and a slew of servants streamed into the room. It seemed as though nearly every member of Langford's female staff was packed into the small bower room.

"Clare, I'd like to speak with my father," she said, edging closer to the one person she knew.

"Not possible, my lady. He and the men are already at the chapel speaking to the priest. We don't have our own, you know. He passed, God rest his soul, a fortnight ago, so we had to borrow one from the village."

At the chapel? Borrow a priest?

What was she to do? Certainly she could air her grievances to her father, but they'd already had that conversation to no avail. She'd hoped to convince Sir Adam to beg out of the wedding, but would he really do that now? Without proper time to hear her complaints?

Nay. Langford was only his because he'd agreed to take her as his wife.

Her hands began to tremble. How could this be happening?

Cora was about to become a stranger's wife.

CHAPTER 3

$\mathcal{T}$he bride had arrived.

Adam dressed carefully that morn. While the actual ceremony was little more than a formality—he and Lord Maxwell had worked out the terms the evening before—his housekeeper had insisted on making it feel like a grand event. She'd declared it would be "the greatest feast Langford has seen in recent times," and she'd helmed a thorough cleaning of the hall these past few days. Though it still didn't look like much, all the old rushes in the hall had been replaced. The few varieties of flowers from Langford's garden had found their way throughout the large room.

For his part, Adam had arranged for the wedding to happen immediately simply because he wished to make it official. He imagined the girl was none too happy about their arrangement despite her father's insistence otherwise. He would not risk anything going wrong. His lordship of Langford, Spencer and Maxwell's plan for establishing some modicum of peace at the border. This marriage had made both possible.

But as he waited with Langford's priest in front of the chapel, he couldn't help but notice Maxwell's expression. The man looked worried. As did his captain, and Adam couldn't ignore how they leaned in toward each other and whispered periodically.

They knew something about her delay. If only he'd had a chance to speak with the lady herself before the event. The fire had been badly timed, but disasters had no respect for schedules. Luckily, the blaze had been put out quickly thanks to the fast thinking of the cobbler, who'd organized a brigade of water buckets.

Something in the warden's manner had concerned him last eve, and it was even more apparent now. So when Adam spotted the small retinue including Clare and two additional handmaidens, he let out a relieved breath.

Until now, he'd given little thought to his bride beyond what she represented. He'd been busy these last few weeks, for Langford had lacked leadership for years. But as the bright green of her dress came into view, he found himself straining to glimpse her face. She walked slowly, moving down the path lined with servants who had stopped their duties to witness the small but important event.

She had red hair.

Not surprising, given her father did as well. But as Lady Cora approached, his eyes

widened. Why had no one deemed it important to mention that his Scottish wife was beautiful? Blood pounded in his ears with every step she took closer to him. She wore no veil or head covering, only a few scattered flowers laced through her long, wavy locks, so he could see every feature.

And there was quite a bit to see.

A large bosom for a petite woman, skin so creamy he itched to know if it felt as smooth as it looked. And her face. Wide, pale-green eyes stared back at him above lips so pink and full, he longed to see them smile. To kiss them. By God, she was perfection.

She also looked desperately unhappy.

Her beauty had so taken him off-guard that it took him a moment to register her mood. But as he looked from her face to her father's, Adam caught the tension between them. *This* was why Maxwell looked so worried. Lady Cora did not want to wed him, and her father knew it.

"My lady."

He bowed and reached out his hand. She didn't move. Would she not take it? Would she refuse him in front of everyone? Her father would never allow it, but Adam knew the consent of both parties was necessary for a wedding to take place. He refused to allow his concern to show.

The priest coughed, and finally—with clear hesitation—Lady Cora took his arm. Aside from the thick gold belt inlaid with deep green sapphires, the lady wore no other jewelry. He'd known plenty of women beneath her station who would take any excuse to adorn themselves with the finest gems they owned, so her forbearance intrigued him.

"My lord."

The huskiness of her voice immediately made him imagine her in his bed. Though Adam had never asked for a wife, especially a Scottish one, the idea suddenly appealed. He would spend each night with this woman, this *beauty*.

He hardly deserved such good fortune.

"Sir Adam Dayne, the first of his name, Lord of Langford...and the Lady Cora Maxwell, daughter of..."

Adam was too busy watching Lady Cora turn the small satchel of herbs in her hand over and over to pay much mind to the ceremony. She was nervous. Mayhap his bride was timid. He knew nothing of her except that she was the daughter of the Scottish warden, a clan chief with a reputation for diplomacy and ferocity matched only by Adam's own overlord. It appeared the daughter was of a different sort. Which was just as well. He desired peace above all else, and a biddable wife would be most welcome.

And yet…why was he disappointed as well? Surely the fiery women he'd always been drawn to would not make ideal wives.

"Congratulations, my lord." Maxwell clapped him on the back.

It was over. He looked at Cora. What an odd notion. She was a stranger, but now she was his wife.

Her expression was inscrutable.

He turned to the crowd that had assembled behind them. "Today is a day for celebration. A holiday for all." He expected the loud cheers and was glad for them.

Oddly, his new wife didn't seem to take kindly to his decree. "You don't approve, my lady?"

He could hardly call the slight curve of her lips a smile.

Her eyes narrowed. "'Tis not my place to say, my lord."

Though the words were kindly spoken, her tone was anything but. A problem for another time. Adam would bring his lovely wife to his side in no time.

He looked forward to the day ahead, as optimistic about his future as he'd ever been. From orphan to…this. A beautiful wife, a castle and demesne any man would be proud to call his own. He owed it all to the earl who had raised him as his own, and he was determined to make him proud.

It was a fine day indeed.

It was the worst day of Cora's life.

Worse than the time her little sister had told one of her potential suitors she was "the coldest fish in the North Sea." Though Lily had only made the hurtful comment because she hadn't wanted Cora to leave her, it had left its mark. And that was before *the incident*.

No matter—now she was married, and to the very man she'd hoped would convince her father this farce was unnecessary.

Granted, he was quite pleasing to the eye, but that hardly mattered.

Cora's father dealt with men from both sides of the border, so she knew more Englishmen than she cared to admit. Which was why she had expected a dandified lord with pointed shoes and a jewel-encrusted cloak to be standing at the entrance of the small chapel.

The first thing she'd noticed about Sir Adam was his height. He was even taller than her father, and his frame was powerful and strong—the body of a man who wasn't afraid of physical work. And then his face had come into view. His brown hair was neither dark nor light, but it was shorter than was fashionable. Beneath that odd cut, he had the most extraordinary hazel eyes. The desire in those eyes had not caught her off-guard— it was the way men typically greeted her—but Cora had most certainly not been prepared for the catch in her breath when he took her arm.

In truth, Sir Adam was the exact opposite of what she'd expected. His surcoat was without embellishments save for a crest that she recognized as Caiser's, and he was no dandy. Though she would not have admitted it aloud, he was undoubtedly the most handsome man she'd ever looked upon.

But none of that mattered. Cora's only thought during the ceremony had been grief for her own powerlessness. For what choice had she been given? Refuse him at the altar, disgrace her family, and return to Scotland to live her life in a convent?

It had hardly seemed like a choice at all, and now it was too late.

She was an Englishman's bride and would live far away from her family, from her clan, from her homeland.

Nay, I will not do it!

"You're quiet, my lady."

As they climbed the steps to the keep, Cora nearly lost her footing. Her husband...husband!...caught her by the arm and steadied her. His grasp was strong.

"I've nothing to say, my lord."

He made no comment. They entered the hall to cheers and made their way toward the dais. Although somewhat bare, the festive atmosphere and smells of the feast made Langford's hall much more inviting than it had been the previous evening.

It did nothing to allay her misery.

Servants carried in trays of food and musicians began to play a tune that was unfamiliar to her. Her father sat next to her, but Cora did not wish to speak to him.

"Adam."

She looked at her husband.

"I am not 'my lord' to you."

"You are a stranger to me," she said.

"I am your husband."

He said it with such conviction and finality that Cora had no choice but to voice her opinion. "That you may be, my lord, but you're a stranger still."

"And if you had your way, would I remain as such?"

His bluntness took her by surprise. She glanced at her father, whose mood seemed to have lightened drastically now that the vows had been exchanged. He was laughing at something his captain had said. At least someone was enjoying the wedding feast.

"Would you like the truth?"

He cocked his head to the side. "I would always have the truth from you, Cora."

Her given name on this stranger's lips should have sounded peculiar, but the way he lowered his voice when he said her name made her feel...odd.

"Aye, it would remain so. If I'd had occasion to speak with you before the ceremony, we could have discussed as much."

He raised his perfectly formed eyebrows. Was there nothing about this man's appearance she could not recommend?

"If you had not retired early, we could have done so."

"If I'd known you planned to rush me to the altar, I would not have retired early."

Cora realized her voice had risen. And while she had plenty to say, she'd not do so within the hearing of a hundred or so guests.

"It matters not, my lord. The deed is done."

Adam picked up his goblet and held it out to her. "Indeed it is, *Cora.*" He smiled and took a sip of the heavily spiced wine.

Cora could smell its contents from where she sat. She should look away. So why did her eyes refuse to shift from his?

Staring back at her, he set the cup down on the table.

She suddenly realized the deed he referred to was not the exchange of their wedding vows. The cad!

"Have I embarrassed you?" he asked.

"Not at all, Sir Adam." She tried to sound experienced. "I do not embarrass easily."

It was actually quite the opposite, but he didn't have to know such a thing.

He leaned toward her, and Cora glanced around, but no one seemed to be paying them any attention.

"Come close, wife."

That rankled. Cora was unused to taking orders, even from her father. This marriage was, of course, the one glaring exception.

"Yes, *husband.*"

His lips were so close to her ear, she could feel his breath on her neck.

Cora shivered.

"I'm pleased to hear that you don't embarrass easily," he whispered. "I believe we will get along well, both in the bedchamber and out of it."

The most unusual feeling deep within her gut prompted her to pull away so quickly, she spilled her own goblet of wine on herself.

"Oh." She attempted to somehow stop the flow of the deep red liquid onto her lap, but it was too late. A servant rushed to the dais and Cora stood, grateful for the excuse to get away from her English husband.

"Can I be of assistance, my lady?" her husband asked. He did not bother to hide the suggestion in his voice. She had to get out of there.

"Pardon me, Sir Adam. Father."

She fairly ran from the hall and allowed the handmaiden to escort her to her chamber.

"Shall I help you choose a new gown, my lady?"

Though the girl appeared fairly young—no more than ten and eight—the half smile upon her lips was unquestionably suggestive. Of course, the youngest of lasses and lads knew *something* of what happened on the wedding night. Cora felt her cheeks grow warm.

The girl chattered happily while she assisted Cora out of the wedding gown, which had likely been stained beyond repair.

An omen?

"A pity, 'tis a fine fabric, my lady." The maid worked quickly to button the back of her fresh gown closed. Most of the dresses she'd brought to Langford were more practical, but her mother had wanted her to have a special gown for her wedding. She, on the other hand, did not care to impress Sir Adam, or anyone really, but...

"We haven't had a lady at Langford since I was a girl."

"Was the previous lord not married?" she asked, her interest piqued in spite of herself.

Or perhaps he'd been a widow?

"Nay, my lady. His wife, God rest her soul and his too, lived in London."

The maid finished her work and Cora turned to face her. She was a pretty girl, with her blonde hair tucked neatly under a serviceable cap.

"They lived separately?"

She'd heard of such a thing, of course. But not as a permanent arrangement. The girl made it sound as if Langford had not had a true mistress in many years.

"Aye, my lady. I ne'er saw her myself. 'Twas not a surprise the lord sired no children."

Which was why Langford had reverted back to its overlord, Cora surmised. And the earl had then bestowed it on her husband.

"How is that possible?"

The maid attempted to brush away the wrinkles in her gown. "*A mensa et thoro*," she said matter-of-factly.

From table and bed. Which meant...

"The lord was abusive?"

In order to legally separate from table and bed—some said from bed and board—a spouse, usually the wife, had to claim abuse. Which was why such a thing was so rare. There was a high tolerance for abuse when it came to a husband and wife.

"Nay, 'tis said he was a most caring man," the girl replied.

That made no sense. "But then—"

"Mistress Clare can tell ye the tale. But as I heard it, she just up and left. Hated it here. Loved London and being at court. We ought not talk about the past on such a happy day. Beggin' my pardon for sayin' so, but you make a beautiful bride, my lady."

Cora had been told she was beautiful her whole life. But it mattered little. To be with her mother and sister, and her father, *that* was what mattered.

"Thank you."

As she walked toward the hall, sounds of talking and laughter floated up to her. When the flutist's sweet melody began, the festive mood emboldened her. A smile surfaced on her face for the first time that day.

It wasn't the wedding feast below that pleased her, but the idea that had taken hold as she talked to the maid. This morning Cora had thought she was well and truly trapped. Shackled to an English knight, left with no recourse except to serve him dutifully as his wife.

But now she had a new plan. One that would allow Sir Adam to keep his English bride and the land and title that went along with it, while also ensuring Cora did not spend her days among strangers hundreds of miles from her country and her family.

It was simple, really.

She may not have had the chance to talk Sir Adam out of the wedding. But as his wife, she would surely have opportunities to force him to set her aside. She'd seen her father easily annoyed with "women's matters." She would simply mimic some of her sister's finer displays.

Children.

If she succeeded in her campaign, Cora would not be able to remarry. She'd never have children of her own. But what was the alternative? Remaining wed to an Englishman?

Never.

Undoubtedly, Sir Adam's confused expression as she walked toward the dais was due to her changed mood. She almost felt sorry for him. For she would do anything to force him to send her home.

And she'd begin her campaign immediately.

CHAPTER 4

*H*is new wife was breathtaking. But she did not want this marriage, which was why the change in her temperament was most unexpected. Who exactly was this new wife of his? Meek, as he first suspected? But that did not qualify with the look in her eye as he teased her earlier.

And now she appeared happy when the woman was anything but earlier in the day.

"I feared you would not return, my lady."

The corners of her mouth lifted. "To my own wedding feast? Whatever would give you such an idea, Adam?"

Instantly, he hardened. A smiling Cora was a sight to behold, and the sound of his name on her lips...

"It seems you've changed more than simply your gown?"

"Forgive me for my earlier temperament. I fear the journey and shock of our hasty nuptials was a bit too much to bear."

He wasn't the only person to notice the change. Lord Maxwell leaned forward to join their conversation. "My dear, you seem... quite happy."

Adam understood his confusion.

"I've changed my gown, Father. And I suddenly feel quite refreshed."

Her father grunted in response, looked quizzically at his daughter, and resumed conversation with his captain.

The meal progressed but Adam hardly noticed the courses being served, though he was very pleased with the cook. Charles may have neglected Langford in some respects, but his slightly rounded belly gave evidence to the fact that its kitchens were well maintained.

"Tell me something about yourself." Cora very delicately picked up a piece of cheese. Adam watched her lips open as she placed the morsel in her mouth. He shifted in his seat.

"What do you want to know?" He wasn't accustomed to idle chatter. The women with whom he'd kept company had consisted mostly of non-nobles or widows—he would never have shamed the Caiser name by bedding a titled, unmarried maid—and none of them had favored conversation of this sort.

"How did you come to forge an alliance with one of the most powerful men along the border?"

He glanced at her father, a man equally as powerful as Spencer. "Luck?"

Cora's laughter sounded like pealing bells. He could get used to such a sound.

"I squired with the earl after both of my parents were killed." He anticipated her next question. "An unknown disease that took four lives in our small manor house and more than twenty others in the village."

Adam rarely spoke of his parents' deaths, and he didn't wish to do so now, especially since his parents' absence on his wedding day was deeply felt. "I had no other family to speak of, and Lord Kenshire raised me like I was his own son. But surely you already know this."

"Aye, my father may have mentioned it."

She scrunched her nose, likely without realizing it. "And you have built quite a reputation at Kenshire."

"Perhaps."

"Perhaps? No man offers such a place," she swept her arm up, "to a retainer. Even members of my clan who stay away from English affairs know of your reputation with the sword."

"It would not surprise me."

Cora's eyes widened. She'd sensed no arrogance in his tone; he simply stated it as a fact.

"And you, Lady Cora?"

"I thought we had dispensed with formalities?"

"My apologies. It's not often I meet a woman and marry her on the same day."

Her smile faltered. She opened her mouth to respond, but closed it instead. *Interesting.* So his wife was choosing to conceal how much she resented the arrangement. *Why?*

"Tell me of your family," he said.

She looked toward her father, who glanced her way and smiled. The man with the fiercest reputation in Scotland appeared remarkably...ordinary at the moment.

"You've met my father," she started, "who refused to allow my mother and younger sister to travel to England for my wedding." She took a sip of wine.

Cora didn't seem upset by her father's decree; she merely stated it as a fact. *Well done, my wife.* He would not remark upon the fact that she likely hoped to return to Scotland.

Their conversation was interrupted by a sound at the back of the hall—a cascading noise that continued to grow louder. Soon, nearly every guest was pounding his or her mug on the trestle tables.

"Are you ready?" Adam whispered to his bride.

She stared blankly back at him. Perhaps they had different traditions where she was from.

"To retire."

Her eyes widened, but he had no time to reassure her. The sound was already deafening. The moment he stood, shouts erupted across the room and the musicians ceased playing.

"Lord Maxwell, honored guests, and all who serve Langford Castle—I thank you for sharing in our celebration here today." More cheers. "As the new lord, I've sworn to protect and care for the people here, and will do so with the diligence instilled in me by the second earl of Kenshire, Spencer Caiser."

He waited for the noise to die down before continuing, pleased by the show of respect for the earl. "I swear the same to my new wife and her family. May God bless them and you on this fine day. And now, we shall retire as man and wife, without witness."

He expected the gasps, but he did not care how anyone else took it—his new wife was visibly relieved. Cora was lovely, even more so with her cheeks slightly flushed from the wine. He held out his hand, and when she stood and laid her delicate fingers on top of his own, Adam could not resist glancing down at her. He felt something that was not normally reserved for man and wife but rather for lovers. Was it possible they could be both? He had never dared hope for such a thing.

He nodded to her father and escorted Cora from the hall amidst bawdy remarks and cheers. They ascended the winding staircase before the noise finally quieted. Adam stopped in front of the lady's temporary quarters. Cora's hand was still tucked in his, and he watched her in the torch-lit hallway, marveling at the play of the light in her vibrant red hair.

The moment ended when Clare ran up to them, breathing heavily.

"My apologies, I was in the kitchens when...where is everyone?"

"I bade them to remain in the hall."

"But, it's your...you'll need to..."

Adam nearly laughed, but Clare had already proven so helpful to him, and he did not want to insult the woman. "You may assist

Lady Cora, Mistress Clare." He bowed to his wife. "I will be waiting for you, my lady."

He turned away before Cora could respond. Her rounded eyes told him what he'd already suspected. His wife was nervous—just as he had been before his first time. He would go slowly and show her the pleasures they could look forward to as husband and wife.

He would tread gently with his nervous new wife.

How could she avoid consummating the marriage?

Her plan to coax Adam to set her aside would never work if they went to bed together. She'd completely forgotten about the barbaric English tradition of the bedding ceremony for nobles. There was no way she could have convinced Adam not to take her fully and truly as his bride if there had been witnesses to the event. Thankfully, he'd set that awful tradition aside, presumably to please her. But it was obvious he still expected to bed her, and she had no clear plan to stop it from happening.

What was she to do? Claim to have her monthly flow? What if that did not stop him? Maidenly embarrassment? She had a feeling it would not work.

There was a quick knock, and then the door within her chamber flew open.

She stood in the middle of the well-appointed bedchamber, complete with a canopied bed and private sitting room. Clare had braided her hair and assisted her into the chemise her mother had sent for this very occasion. The material was so thin, it was nearly transparent. A fact she was reminded of as she watched Adam's face.

"I worried you may have forgotten it was your wedding night."

She would focus on his face. Cora refused to look down at his bare...

Dear Lord.

Dressed only in braies, the man was as solid as the stone wall behind him. The soft glow of the fire revealed every muscle. Every line. She could not look away from his stomach. She'd seen men train shirtless but never, not once, had she seen a man's stomach look quite so… Cora wanted desperately to touch the muscles there.

No, she did not! What she wanted was to escape the evening with her virginity.

"'Twould be hard to forget. Adam."

He turned, closed the heavy wooden door as if it were a piece of parchment, and walked toward her. In just a few strides, her husband stood so close she could smell his scent, a combination of clover and leather. Some instinct made her breathe in deeply.

Then he reached for her and she panicked.

"Your stomach!"

His hand stayed.

"It's so…muscular." Cora knew she sounded ridiculous, but they had been the first words to come to mind. Perhaps if she delayed long enough, she could hope for divine intervention.

"I am a knight," he said simply.

"I've seen knights train before." She turned and walked toward the fire, rubbing her hands as if cold. In truth, she was anything but. "But I've never seen anything quite like it."

She didn't have to turn around to sense his approach. His body exuded an unmistakable warmth and presence.

"I would hope not."

What is that *supposed to mean?*

"Tell me more about yourself, my lord…Adam."

She waited, but he remained silent. Moments later, she heard retreating footsteps and then the sound of the door opening once again. He was gone? Could it have been that easy? Excitement bubbled inside her. He didn't like to talk about himself. Well, she would do nothing but ask questions.

It would seem she had celebrated too soon.

Adam walked back through the door a moment later with two goblets and a flagon of wine. He set them on a nearby table and poured two drinks. Handing one to her, he took a deep swig of his own.

"Drink, Cora."

Although it sounded more like a command than she would have liked, Cora did so anyway. The sweet French wine felt smooth flowing down her throat.

He moved two chairs from the sitting room, arranging them by the fire. They were ornate, high-backed chairs with crimson and gold cushions. "Sit."

Was she a dog to be ordered about so? Cora nearly asked the question aloud, but then she remembered her purpose.

She sat and pulled her legs up beneath her. Cora caught him looking at her bare calves, and a jolt of desire ran through her and settled between her legs. It was the oddest sensation.

"You're nervous."

She was, but not for the reason he assumed. Or, at least, not only for that reason.

"Aye, very much so." She cast her eyes downward in the way she'd seen her sister, a more practiced flirt, do a thousand times. Cora had no use for such silly affectations. Before he'd sold her off in marriage, her father had brought home dozens of eligible bachelors in the hopes of enticing her to marriage. While her sister had chased every last one of them, Cora had continued to spend her free time learning to hunt and shoot the longbow. Perhaps that was what had gotten her here.

And now that she was married, Cora had no doubt her sister would find a suitor without haste. And then her mother would be alone with only a man who was more companion than husband. A man who cared more for making war, and peace, than he did for his wife.

"The wine will help," Adam offered.

She took a sip and looked up, giving her half-naked husband a most pitiful look. "It's just... I would very much like to get to know you first. Before we...you know. I would be so much more relaxed if it weren't for..."

She did not dare look into his eyes, but it was easy to imagine the look in them. As the fire crackled beside her, Cora held her breath...waiting. Lord help her, she could not stop looking at his chest. The muscles there twitched. She lifted her head, finally, and watched as his frown softened.

"How long do you imagine it will take for us to 'become acquainted' with one another?"

Yes!

This was important. If she answered too long a time period, he would scoff at her request. Too short, and she would not have time to convince him to send her home.

She took a deep breath. "A fortnight."

Adam nearly spat out his wine.

"Think on it, my lord! Most couples are well acquainted, betrothed for years. They've become accustomed to the idea while I...well...I just learned of this marriage a few weeks ago. I'd never even heard of my future husband before. And we just met this morn. Wouldn't it be much more enjoyable if we were both comfortable?

He looked anything but comfortable at the moment. In fact, he looked like he wanted to break something.

"Please?" She blinked and opened her eyes wide.

"A fortnight," he said.

But before she could respond, he added, "And if, at the end of that time, you don't feel properly 'acquainted,' we will get to know each other another way. As husband and wife."

His meaning was clear. She had no alternative but to acquiesce.

"Aye, I agree." She smiled, relaxed for the first time all evening. "Don't you feel so much better?"

"Nay, I do not."

But he didn't move. Cora had expected him to leave now that they'd finalized their agreement, but instead he stood, refilled his cup, and walked toward her with the flagon. She lifted her goblet, and he filled it nearly to the top.

"To our marriage." Cora was feeling generous.

Adam, still surly, lifted his cup and drank deeply.

"What was it like, growing up at Kenshire?" she asked.

Cora was genuinely curious about the English earl who'd earned her father's respect. And she knew from her father men typically did not endure endless questions well.

Adam leaned back, stretching and crossing his legs in front of him. Even they were muscled. Finely so.

"I have no complaints."

"That's all you have to say? You have no complaints?"

He raised his eyebrows. "Nay, I do not."

Oh, for heaven's sake. It would be a long fortnight if this was his manner of carrying on a conversation. "Tell me about the earl."

"Why so curious? Most Scots would not trouble themselves to know so much."

"I am not most Scots. My father has been brokering for peace along the border with your English earl for as long as I can remember." She tried to keep the bitterness out of her voice.

"He is a fine man. None finer, truth be told. It is an honor to serve him—and even more so to have been given such a high position in his household."

"Raised like a son."

Adam's face softened, if only a little. "Aye. He has given me everything, and I shall do the same for him."

So her husband was fiercely loyal to his overlord. As he should be.

"And Sir Richard?"

He smiled broadly, his white teeth visible even in the semi-darkness. Her heart hammered in her chest. No matter how she willed herself not to react to him, these new feelings were not so easily controlled.

"If I could have chosen a brother, it would have been Richard. I've yet to meet a man or maid not instantly enamored with him."

"I would imagine the same is said about you." She had *not* intended to say that.

Adam leaned forward, watching her with those dizzying hazel eyes.

"You have no natural siblings?" she asked, almost too quickly.

He didn't want to talk about it. And for a moment, Cora thought he would not answer her question.

"Aye, a sister who died in childbirth. My mother nearly did not survive."

His features softened.

"She was not quite the same afterwards. Still kind and gentle. I remember her fondly. But not the same as before my sister was born."

Adam stopped talking as abruptly as he started. "I have not spoken those words aloud before," he said.

"I should not have asked."

His gaze did not waver. "Aye, you should have. You are my wife. There shall be no secrets between us." Adam reached out to set down his goblet. Then he stood and grabbed her hand so fast she nearly spilled her wine.

Before she knew what he intended, Adam had pulled her so close they nearly touched.

"But you promised!" He could not do this. If he kept pursuing her, she would bend to him—she felt herself leaning closer to him even now—and she would be stuck in England forever.

"Relax, my nervous little dove. I do not break a promise. You shall remain a maid this eve."

Her shoulders sank and she tried to breathe normally.

Adam took her hand as he'd done in the hall, but this time he brought it to his lips.

"But you said nothing of this." He kissed the top of her hand and then turned it around. Cora could see the green flecks in the light brown of his eyes as he continued to watch her. "Or this." He kissed her wrist and flicked his tongue against it.

That feeling again, deep inside her. Like the flutter of a butterfly's wings.

Cora knew she should pull away—her plan depended on it—but she could not.

In one swift motion, he released her hand and pulled her even closer. She had no further warning before Adam lowered his head and placed his lips on hers. She wasn't sure what to do.

"Open your mouth for me, Cora."

"Open my—"

He lowered his head again and covered her lips with his own. His hands cupped her face, holding her in place. And then she felt his tongue.

What is he doing?

As if he could hear her silent question, he touched his tongue to hers and showed her what to do. Cora could not summon the will to make him stop. Nay, she didn't *want* him to stop.

And then *he* pulled away from *her*. Had she done something wrong? Cora nearly asked the question aloud before she caught herself. She stepped back, still breathing heavily.

"A fortnight," he said, then abruptly turned and walked out of her chamber.

What had just happened?

This was not the way to convince him to set her aside. Tomorrow, she would do better.

CHAPTER 5

*T*hree days had passed since the wedding, and Cora was miserable.

Her father had left the day before, along with the rest of the contingent from her clan. And while Cora was grateful for Clare, who had done everything possible to make her feel welcome, she missed her own handmaiden. Missed the companionship of her mother and sister.

Missed her home.

She nearly opened the letter her mother gave her, but something stopped her. She didn't need to read it. Cora would be going home to see her mother, and they could talk about the letter's contents.

Though none were outright rude to her here, Cora sensed a certain wariness from the servants. They treated her with respect, but with the exception of Clare, most looked at her as if she were, well, Scottish.

And then there was Adam.

While he made no mention of their agreement, he continued to visit her each night after she retired for the evening. As many questions as she asked, Adam answered openly and without resentment. She was beginning to think he did not mind their conversations and reluctantly admired his genuine interest in their companionship. Luckily, the incident on the evening of the wedding had not been repeated. Even so, she awoke each morning with a tingling on her lips, thinking of that kiss.

She was glad he had not tested her will again.

Now that her father was no longer a witness, Cora planned to begin her campaign to end her marriage. Although she rose early, Adam had already broken his fast and left the hall. He spent his days training, inspecting the land, and visiting Langford's village. Which boded well for her plan.

"Charles," she said to the steward who had just entered the hall, "will you show me the property this morning?"

The steward's shoulder-length white hair reminded Cora of her grandfather. Her memories of the man were mostly faded, but she remembered the vivid stories he used to tell the children by the hearth and how he'd always chuck her under the chin.

"It would be my pleasure, my lady."

Charles left to speak with a man Cora didn't recognize, a knight by the look of him, and returned just as she finished her meal.

They spent most of the day inspecting every room in the castle and its gardens. But there was one particular area of interest for her today—the kitchen. She knew, unlike the past few days, Adam planned to be present for the mid-day meal. Luckily, the cook was more than happy to accommodate her request for "a course that reminded her of home."

Dressed in a simple, pale-blue day gown, her hair unbound— as was her custom—Cora greeted Adam with a smile when he arrived at the great hall for the busiest meal of the day.

He had arrived just in time to enjoy Cook's creation.

"Good afternoon, my lady."

"Sir Adam."

"Ale, if you please," he instructed the serving woman, who handed him a bowl of cullen stink soup.

Cora watched as he distractedly lifted his spoon to his mouth. Though she was eager to watch him, she tried not to stare, shifting her gaze instead to a group of knights sitting beneath them at the well-worn trestle tables. One stared back, and he looked none too pleased.

"What in God's name..."

Adam's face had twisted into a pucker. Most of those who'd tried the soup, not accustomed to its bitter taste, were making much the same face.

"Is something amiss, my lord?"

He pushed aside the first course and reached for a hunk of bread.

"Aye, I've not tasted anything so foul since—"

"Yes?" she asked sweetly, letting herself look at him.

Dressed in nothing more than hose and a loose linen shirt, Adam looked every bit like a man who had spent his morning in the training yard. His hair was more disheveled than usual. He'd covered himself up on all of his evening visits since their wedding night, but Cora couldn't help but think of what lay underneath the thin cloth of his shirt.

"Cora?"

She'd been caught staring.

"Do you have some insight into today's menu?"

She tasted the soup and was quite impressed by its quality.

"Do you like it?"

If she looked at him, she'd surely laugh. She didn't want Adam to know she had deliberately sabotaged him.

"Like it?" He pointed to the dozen or so men eating bread and cheese as they waited for the next course. "What do you think?"

She feigned injury, giving him a pouty look. "It's considered a

delicacy back home. Surely you wouldn't deny me some famil-
iarity with my homeland?"

He pushed the bowl away.

"Odd. I had understood the border customs to be much like
our own."

"If you'll remember, my lord, we are no longer at the border.
It's less than two full days' ride to London."

Adam's face looked as if he'd taken another taste of the soup.

"You don't like London?"

He shook his head. "Having been raised in Northumbria, I
prefer the country. Langford suits me well."

It did not suit her at all, but Cora remained silent. She reluctantly agreed with his preference for a more simple life. Her
impression from the Scottish nobles she interacted with left much
to be desired.

"Then you won't mind that I've asked Charles to send for a
tailor?" She hurried to continue. "Rather than travel to London, I
could be fitted for a new wardrobe here, at Langford."

Cora had no use for new gowns, but Adam need not
know that.

"I...of course. I will be looking at accounts this afternoon."

She feigned delight. "Oh, I do love assisting with the household
accounts. Where shall I meet you? In the solar?"

At home, her father had never allowed her to manage such
things even though she could read and write. The suggestion was
highly irregular, and Cora knew Adam would be none too pleased
with the prospect, especially since she'd implied she liked to spend
money as a sport.

Which was why she had suggested it.

"You understand, of course, that embedded jewels are quite
popular at the moment. Not just as adornments but all
throughout the gown."

Cora didn't give Adam an opportunity to answer.

"When we do attend court, there will be a higher standard for me. Being Scottish and all. We must travel to London eventually, you know."

She smiled brightly and almost felt sorry for her poor husband, who looked more than a bit dismayed.

Cora stood. "I shall meet you and Charles shortly. Until then."

He simply stared at her.

Cora nearly ran from the hall before he could deny her request. She walked so quickly that she ran straight into a messenger being escorted toward Adam. The dusty young man, who clearly had traveled some distance to reach Langford, offered his apologies and made his way to the lord, accompanied by Charles.

She stopped to watch the exchange for a moment and then exited the hall. Though she didn't intend to remain at Langford, Cora planned to speak to the head gardener. She figured the least she could do for the kindness Clare—and, yes, Adam—had shown to her here was to leave her mark on the paltry assortment of flowers that was Langford's garden. Though the herbs and spices were plentiful, no ornamental flowers or greenery softened the approach to the keep's entrance.

She planned to rectify that when she wasn't busy planning ways to make Adam's life miserable.

Cora was making his life hell. The sweet, comely maid he married was proving to be a bit of a hoyden. To be fair, "sweet" may never have been the right word to describe his wife.

First, her ridiculous insistence on waiting to consummate their marriage. Adam had made more than one visit to the nearby river to take a cold swim to douse his ever-growing desire for the Scottish lass now occupying the room adjacent to his own. Her sudden fascination with attending court. Her fascination with being gowned in the height of fashion. Then she had insisted on attending his meeting with Charles after that horrible lunch she'd arranged with Cook. Cora had asked dozens of questions, making it damn near impossible for them to get anything accomplished.

He should have told her to leave. But she'd reminded him earlier that she had been displaced from her home, and Adam wanted her to know she had a new one. Ultimately, he'd left the task to his wife and steward.

He'd spent the remainder of the day inspecting buildings and hadn't returned to the keep until after dark. All day, his thoughts had been fixed on the messenger who'd arrived earlier in the day from Kenshire. Richard was on his way to Langford. He would arrive as early as the following morning. Though he always welcomed a visit from his friend, his *brother*, Richard could not know that he and Cora had not yet consummated their marriage. There was the rub: Richard, more astute than most, would immediately guess that something was amiss.

Now, after the evening meal, which was laden with Scottish delicacies, he stood in his bedchamber waiting for Cora. No doubt she would not be happy to hear of their altered sleeping arrangements. Well, he was not happy about the prospect of never again eating a decent meal in his own home.

The door within his chamber creaked open.

"My lord, you asked to see me?"

The hour was late, but the fire and the candles arranged throughout the chamber cast warm light on his wife.

He could not do it. He couldn't possibly sleep next to her while keeping his word...

Adam smiled at the stricken look on her face.

"I promise not to ravish you the moment you step inside." He smirked. "Although I cannot apologize for looking at you as if I might do just that."

She remained at the threshold.

"Come in, Cora. I'll explain." He held out a goblet of wine, pleased when she stepped forward to accept it. His hand brushed her hip as he moved to close the door.

"You must stay here tonight."

Rather than comment, she glided past him. "Your chamber is larger than I imagined it would be."

That she had imagined this bedchamber at all was encouraging.

"It seems Langford's original owners had a predilection for privacy. The solar is a

separate chamber, as you know. This room is used primarily for sleeping."

"Why?"

"Why is it used for sleeping, or why are you here?" He knew the answer she sought but wanted to get her mind off the fact that she stood within his reach in nothing more than a chemise. Though not as thin as the one she had worn on their wedding night, it nonetheless left little to his imagination.

"You say you'll keep your word, so why must I sleep here?"

She was nervous.

He sat on the edge of the bed, its thick coverlet and feather mattress sinking under his weight. "Richard is coming." He drank deeply from his goblet, the smooth spiced wine a welcome relief.

"I don't understand."

He didn't want to explain it to her. Adam didn't want to talk at all. He wanted to pull his wife onto the bed and make love to her. He wanted to feel the overabundant breasts that peeked out from beneath the thin piece of fabric that was the only barrier between his hands and her naked body.

He wanted Cora more than he'd ever wanted a woman. Ironic that he'd had an easier time bedding women who were *not* his wife.

"He cannot know about our 'arrangement.'"

"Hmm." She turned and moved closer to the fire. While the

room was not as large as most great chambers, its stone fireplace was an impressive structure.

Adam now had a perfect view of her impressive backside.

"What would happen if he knew?"

Her red hair looked as if it were on fire. He certainly was. Adam couldn't take much more of this temptation.

"He would tease me mercilessly. Worse, he may carry the tale back to Spencer." And that was to be avoided at all costs. He'd never before disappointed the earl, and it would chafe if the first time it happened was because he'd failed in this—consummating his marriage with the beautiful woman standing before him.

Yet understanding this woman felt more challenging than the countless battles he'd endured at the earl's side, the three times he'd nearly lost his life in battle, and even the Day of Truce. It was becoming clear she intended to push him away. But this was one battle he didn't intend to lose.

"I will stay here—" Cora turned to him, "—for a boon."

"A boon? Woman, what in God's name are you talking about?"

"You need not raise your voice."

"My wife is bartering to sleep in my bed! I'd say I have cause to raise my voice."

There were men on the battlefield who had turned and run when he'd spoken to them in this very tone. But not her. Timid? How could he have thought it for an instant?

"One additional week. It's all I ask for. To get to know you."

This was absurd. What game was she playing at?

He was too tired to untangle her motives tonight.

"Fine."

He placed his goblet on the small wooden table near the bed and began to undress.

"What are you doing?" Eyes wide, Cora looked at him as if he'd just told her the king of England was coming for a visit on the morrow.

Adam removed his tunic and slipped off the hose underneath.

He laughed when Cora nearly tripped from turning around so quickly. He contemplated waiting for her to turn back around before getting into bed, but he'd likely have to wait all night. He meant for her to understand the terms of their new agreement started immediately.

"Good night, Cora." She gave him a quick glance over her shoulder—those green eyes flashing above her pink lips—and that was his last sight of his wife before he settled onto the mattress.

Though relieved when he finally felt Cora's weight on the bed, Adam resigned himself to a sleepless night. At least she had agreed to keep their ridiculous agreement discreet. Normally he would be overjoyed by the prospect of seeing Richard, but under the current circumstances, he wished the visit could be delayed.

"Tell me more of him."

Adam rolled to his side to find Cora so close to the edge of the bed it was a wonder she didn't topple to the ground below. Her head lay delicately on the feather pillow as her hands kept busy braiding hair that she'd swept to the side. He watched her nimble fingers make quick work of the long tresses.

She clearly tried to annoy him with her questions. Unfortunately for her, it was not working. "Who?"

She turned toward him.

"Richard."

Though the coverlet was pulled to her chin, Adam could still see the shape of her breasts underneath. He tried to concentrate on her face instead. It was a face meant to be held. To be cherished.

What an odd notion. He clearly needed sleep.

"He is nearly identical to his father in both looks and temperament. Both are intelligent, a mite stubborn, and fiercely loyal."

"Loyal to their men, you mean?"

"To everyone."

She made an unladylike noise. He didn't need to ask her what it meant to know she was skeptical of his claim.

"My apologies. It's just...an Englishman. Fiercely loyal? Even to a woman?"

"Cora, I know you haven't much experience with Englishmen—"

"And how would you know such a thing?" She sat up and Adam groaned. She seemed too agitated to realize what she had done, but he was perfectly aware.

His hands ached to reach out and feel the fullness of her breasts. He took a deep breath.

It would be a long night indeed.

"I know because your father told me the evening before our wedding. He warned you might have some...difficulty...with the transition."

He wasn't sure she would appreciate her father's exact words. He had said, "The stubborn chit harbors more resentment for the English than most members of our clan. Never mind that I've worked for years to broker peace along the border. She has a mind of her own, and no accounting where she gets such ideas."

Adam had some notion of where Cora's stubborn streak may originate.

"I have as much experience with Englishmen as you likely have with Scottish women."

Adam could not concentrate on their conversation. The astonishing fact was that, despite how she'd tormented him, he wanted his wife.

Badly.

"I doubt that very much."

He had said it without thinking, not accustomed to speaking so freely with a member of the opposite sex.

Cora crossed her arms in front of her, pressing up her breasts. His ornery temptress; his bed nymph.

"Tell me."

Her words and tone, even the face she made as she crossed her arms and glared at him, cautioned him to reconsider the tale, which was not fit for a lady's ears.

Nay. Mayhap she would do well to understand he was, to some, a worthy catch.

"During one of Lord Kenshire's meetings at the border—"

"With my father."

"Yes, with your father and clan, I met a Scottish widow who did not seem bothered by my heritage. In fact, she was fascinated by the fact that we were English."

"And?"

His bed nymph was mighty impatient.

"And I believe it is time for us both to get some rest. Good night, lady wife."

He turned from her, shifting his concentration to the fire still crackling in the corner of their chamber, trying not to feel the distant warmth of her. He would wait until she had fallen asleep before he added another log to the fire.

"What happened?"

Lord, save him.

"I came to know her, and she realized her mistake. Good night."

"Came to know her?" There was a hint of genuine interest, mixed with…something else.

She was his wife. And she would eventually come to learn of such things. Lady Cora Maxwell was an innocent, but she was also a married woman. His married woman.

He turned toward her and took a deep breath.

"We stayed at Archbald Castle. Your father had already returned for home, but Richard and I were asked to remain. This particular widow traveled with her uncle and…"

He stopped.

She waited.

"She expressed an interest in me." As Cora was doing now.

She leaned toward him, likely without realizing it. Winning

47

over his wife may be a difficult task, but it would not be an impossible one.

If he were a gentleman, he would refuse to continue. But he was her husband, damn it.

"I took her to my bed. Spent the better part of the evening instructing her on the difference between the Scotsmen to whom she was accustomed and the Englishman who—"

He did stop then. His wife should have been insulted he spoke so openly about another woman. Instead, she looked...intrigued. Adam shifted toward her. Cora may not want to consummate their marriage, but he could tell she did want him.

And he aimed to prove it.

"Who was intent on seducing her," he finished. Cora sat as still as a knight being dubbed. She watched him closely, the mistrust in her eyes evident.

"Shall I show you, Cora?"

"How you seduced another woman? I think not."

"Nay, my love. How I will seduce you." He traced the outline of her shoulder with his finger and then ran it down the length of her thin chemise. He grazed the soft material gently, careful not to touch her skin.

He'd been an idiot.

While it was true the woman in his bed was sworn to him for life, she was right—they had only just met. Perhaps she did need time to acclimate to England. To him.

"You miss your home, Cora." It was not a question, but Cora answered anyway.

She swallowed. "Very much. Our countries are similar in many ways, but they are also very different. My father is a patriot. Taught me to love my clan, my country. And I do. It's here." She pointed to her heart.

Something occurred to him.

"You will see your home again. We can visit as often as possible. You know that, aye?"

48

He could tell from her expression she did not.

Adam needed to convince her another way. Perhaps she needed to be shown how to respond to the desire she obviously felt for him.

He would seduce his own wife. And he would start immediately.

CHAPTER 6

My love.
        It had been said so casually, so naturally, Cora didn't think Adam even realized the words had left his lips. And he seemed so sincere when he said they could visit her home. Something stirred in her. Something frightening and primal. For the briefest of moments, she wanted it to be true. Wanted a marriage unlike her parents' polite but loveless relationship.

But this wasn't love she was feeling. It was simple desire. And if he didn't stop touching her like that, Cora wasn't sure if she'd be strong enough to resist.

Her husband was incredibly handsome, and she also felt... drawn to him. This arrangement, sleeping here in his bed—nay, *their* bed—was not going to work.

"Adam, I don't think—"

He finally touched his fingers to her bare flesh, sweeping them along her neck and across her chest. His casual position, propped on one elbow, was at odds with his expression.

Adam looked up at her with such intensity that Cora found she could not speak. She felt the fingers dip lower, beneath the opening of her cream-colored undergarment. He sat up then, the bed cover falling to reveal the muscles she desperately wanted to touch. But she couldn't speak. Or move.

With one tug at the string that gathered the material of her chemise together, Adam allowed himself greater access. He pulled the chemise down over one shoulder and resumed where he had left off. Everywhere his powerful hands touched felt like flicks of the fire's flames on her skin. She could not, would not, ask him to stop.

He lifted his chin as if signaling something important was about to happen.

And it did.

He reached over and took her full breast in his hand. His groan reverberated inside her. Cora's eyes drifted shut.

"Adam."

His thumb brushed her nipple.

"Cora."

He splayed his hand over the hardened peak and cupped her again. And then his warm, calloused soldier's hand was gone.

Her eyes flew open.

"Lay back."

Another command. One would never guess this man was not the earl's actual son by birth.

"Nay."

Forget her vows. She could not play the passive maid any longer, and it was time her husband realized as much.

"I will not be commanded, husband."

He didn't hesitate. "Very well. Will you lay back so I can pleasure you?"

A shiver ran down her body. "Pleasure me? You already…that is to say…our agreement."

He rolled his eyes and looked endearingly playful when he did so.

"You will remain a virgin, Cora. As I told you before, I do not break my word."

"And I don't believe you any more now than I did then." She said it without thinking. But her words were not exactly true. She did believe him.

Rather than respond, he lowered himself back onto his elbow, and Cora felt herself sliding closer to him.

"Lower," he said.

And this time she listened.

"Close your eyes."

"Adam, I—"

"Although it should not be so—we are, after all, man and wife —you have my word, Cora. I will not take your virginity...this night."

For tonight, she chose to believe him. For tonight, she chose to trust him.

Cora closed her eyes in anticipation, waiting, waiting, and... nothing. She listened to Adam's steady breathing. A loud crackle startled her eyes open. The fire roared in its hearth. Adam raised his eyebrows and she slammed her eyes shut again.

Still, nothing, until she finally felt the cool air waft against her side as he slid his hand beneath the coverlet. Adam's hand traced her hip and the length of her thigh.

"Relax, love."

She was trying to do just that. But Cora had not expected to find herself in her husband's bed, his hands wreaking havoc on her senses, only a week into their agreement.

Why was he so focused on her leg?

Cora would have asked that very question, but she decided it did not matter. The feather-soft touch made her ache for more. For what...she wasn't sure.

And suddenly, his hand was *there*.

"Nay, don't," he whispered as Cora immediately shifted to close her legs.

His hand paused in its perusal and lay still on her most inti-mate parts.

And then he slipped a finger inside and Cora thought she would die of embarrassment. Until he began to move, circling and pressing. Pure sensation shot through her body, making her shake.

"I want you to keep your eyes closed. Can you do that, Cora?"

"Aye," she moaned out.

Another loud crackle startled her.

"Listen to me," he said. "I'm going to pleasure you."

What could that mean? But there was no need to ask, for he was quick to show her. His hand pressed against her as he slipped another finger inside. She pushed against him, not understanding but wanting so much more.

"Your body is mine. You are mine. And I claim both, now."

Another command. But at this moment, she wanted it to be true.

Cora arched her back, meeting his wonderful fingers as they moved in and out until a shudder ran from her core up the length of her body. Her eyes flew open, the feeling so intense and startling, it scared her. She let out a slow, deep breath.

"I…"

No words seemed sufficient.

Adam leaned down to place his lips on hers. So gently that for a moment, albeit a brief one, she thought perhaps…

Nay, he simply desired her.

Maybe one kiss would not hurt.

His lips coaxed hers open, and when they did, his tongue immediately slipped inside. She touched her own to his and was lost.

He had never withdrawn his hand! And then the onslaught began in truth.

She tried to talk, to ask about what he was doing, but he deepened the kiss, his tongue and fingers moving in harmony with one another. When she moaned, Adam pulled her even closer. She reached around him and placed a hand tentatively on his back.

Muscles constricted under her fingers. It was as if she had grabbed ahold of a rock, hard and smooth but warm and alive.

It was simply too much.

She exploded, pressing into him shamelessly. The sound that escaped her was so deep, Cora could hardly believe it was her own.

He pulled away so suddenly it took her a moment to realize he was standing. The quick glimpse of his backside confirmed her husband was indeed leaving. He grabbed a garment from a trunk at the foot of the massive bed—she couldn't tell what it was—and walked toward the door.

"Get some rest, Cora."

And then he was gone.

Rest? Is he jesting? She could no sooner sleep now than forget she was the wife of an Englishman. Despite what had happened, she still planned on leaving. Cora did not belong here. And when Sir Richard arrived tomorrow, it would be the perfect opportunity for her to show Adam they were unsuitable.

What had passed between them this night was desire. Nothing more.

Wasn't it?

Adam sat in his solar. Earlier, he'd thought seducing her was a worthy plan, but he now wondered at the wisdom of that decision. After a brisk walk along the ramparts, he'd returned to find Cora fast asleep in the middle of his bed.

The sight of her had been so enticing, he'd had to leave.

He wasn't sure he understood what had happened between them this eve, only that his wife had brought him to the brink of pleasure with nothing more than her own release.

Why?

She was neither docile nor biddable. Cora Maxwell was quite

the opposite. A woman who bristled at taking orders and was intelligent enough to convince the people around her to do her bidding. One who possessed an unharnessed passion she didn't even know existed.

And while the staff, with the exception of Clare and perhaps Charles, was leery of a Scottish mistress, Langford's new lady had ingrained herself in their lives with abandon. She was proving to be quite expensive, however, and the havoc she'd wreaked on the menu today had left his men begging that he speak to her, to Cook, or both.

"My lord?"

Adam must have fallen asleep. It was rare, and extremely disconcerting, that he had not heard Charles enter the room.

"Your guests have arrived."

Adam wore only hose and a linen shirt. He looked out the small shuttered window barely aglow with light. "Has the fast been broken yet, Charles?"

"Nay, my lord."

Richard had arrived early—not a great surprise since his friend so often traveled at night.

"I will be down to greet them in a moment." He stood and walked toward the door leading to his bedchamber. He was glad he'd insisted on having no servants assist him. Now, he could speak to Cora alone before going downstairs to greet Richard.

She was still sleeping.

Adam didn't know how long he stood at the foot of the bed watching his bride. One shapely leg was thrown over the coverlet, and he ached to run his hand along it. To explore her body and make her his wife in truth.

Nay, this was not the time for them to reach a new understanding. He had to get out of here. With any luck, Cora would remember his desire not to alert Richard that anything was amiss. He slipped on a simple short tunic and then walked down the winding staircase.

"Look who's come to greet us? If it isn't the Lord of Langford himself."

Adam smiled as he approached the small retinue at the other end of the hall. While the servants hurried to move the trestle tables from their nighttime position along the edges of the room, preparing for an earlier than normal morning meal, Adam greeted his guests.

"Perhaps if you'd chosen to arrive at a reasonable hour, you would have received a grander reception." He nodded at Richard's retainers, none of whom he recognized, and embraced his friend, who slapped his back with the strength of two men.

"The sun is ready to rise, 'tis a fine time for a walk, aye?" Richard said.

Adam turned to Charles, who was standing up straight with his hands clasped in front of him. A swelling of fondness caught him off-guard—he'd enjoyed working with the older man these last weeks.

"Please make these men comfortable until it's time to break their fast."

"Of course, my lord." Charles indicated the men should follow while Adam was left alone with Richard.

"How goes it, brother?" Richard asked as they stepped outside.

Adam pointed to the sun, which had just begun to show itself in the distance. They quieted, watching as the vibrant colors of dawn replaced the darkness.

"I don't deserve all that your father has given me," he said seriously.

Richard's expression didn't change. They watched as the drawbridge was lowered for the wagons that brought supplies to the castle each morning. Without a master, Langford had remained functional, but it could be something so much more than that. Adam hoped to make it the home he'd always desired—with his wife.

"You speak so seriously, brother. I can only hope you don't mean it."

With nearly the same height and build, anyone who heard their endearment would have no cause to think them anything but brothers. That Richard wore his hair to his shoulders, in the more fashionable style, was the only way some could tell them apart from a distance.

"Do you remember the morning our camp was attacked before we had time to prepare?" Adam asked.

"The first and only battle I've attended with no clothing. I had two swords at the ready that morn," Richard answered.

They laughed at the shared memory of Richard emerging from the tent stark naked, sword in hand. Adam had no doubt his friend would have entered the skirmish in such a state if necessary.

"You saved me that day," Richard sobered.

"Nay, you would have seen the man's battle ax well before he used it to slice your skull open."

"Mayhap. But one will never know."

Adam said nothing.

"My father is ill."

It took a moment for Adam to understand what Richard had just said—another for him to manage to speak. He'd never heard his friend sound so grave.

"Ill?"

"Spitting up blood when he thinks no one notices. I spoke to his physician myself."

Adam looked at Richard's profile. His normally affable face was drawn. Goddammit. Spencer was dying.

So, *this* was the reason Richard had traveled south. Not to congratulate him on his marriage but to inform him the earl was dying. He couldn't account for it.

"You'll come to my wedding with your new wife?" Richard asked.

"Of course, Richard. I will do anything you ask of me."

Adam lifted his face into the cool morning air, trying to collect himself. An impossible task after hearing about the grave illness of the man who had given him a new life after he'd lost everything.

"I know," Richard said. "I wanted you to hear the news from me."

"I should be there." Adam didn't belong in the south of England enjoying his new life while Spencer's health failed and Richard navigated the succession of the title. He had advisors, of course, but none who would tell him bluntly when he made a mistake.

"Nay, you belong here. My father wants to secure the border more than anything. Trouble brews with the Scots, and he hasn't spent his life building Kenshire to see his legacy come crumbling to the ground. He needs you. To ensure there will always be a place of safety for his family...my family."

"But your family has many holdings."

"*Our* family has only one far away from the troublesome borders," Richard countered.

"I will not let you down."

If Adam lived another one hundred years, he would not know a more fierce yet loyal man than his friend. Richard was about to become one of the most powerful men in England. The earl of Kenshire, once a seat of the Northumbrian kings, wielded as much power as nearly any in the land save the King. He certainly looked the part: his black tunic was inlaid with the Caiser crest, a silver-lined mermaid at its center, the effect almost regal.

Most importantly, Richard was a good man, one who would not lead them into battle over a trifle, no matter how tense the situation along the border. Adam would follow him to the gates of heaven...or hell.

Richard clasped his shoulder. "I know you will not. Now come,

I'd like to meet the woman who must endure your stubborn countenance for all her days."

They made their way back down to the hall, where all remnants of early morn had vanished. The staff had transformed the normally simple fare into a feast worthy of a king.

It was then that Adam noticed the smell. It wasn't the savory allure of food and drink but a delicate scent of sweet lavender. Then he noticed the flowers. They were everywhere—all kinds of them.

Clare escorted them to the dais. "Do you like the flowers, my lord?"

"Aye, mistress. You—"

"Cora. She and the gardener picked every flower on the estate, I believe, and planted even more. But it smells wondrous, does it not?"

"Wondrous indeed."

Where is Cora?

No sooner had the thought entered his head than the woman herself entered the hall, looking every bit the lady of the manor. He had gotten used to the fiery red tresses falling in waves around her shoulders. But this morning it was pulled into an elaborate plait behind her. Courtesy of Clare?

Her dress was simple, but it was embroidered around the neckline and the arms, and cut lower than the others he'd seen on her thus far. She looked both like an innocent maid and a delicate angel who'd come to ease all his troubles.

She was neither.

They stood. "My lady, may I introduce Sir Richard Caiser, son of Spencer Caiser, second earl of Lancaster. Sir Richard, my wife, Lady Cora Maxwell, daughter of—"

"You can dispense with the formalities. We all know the attempt on my life is what forced this marriage. She is the sacrificial lamb offered to you to keep the peace between our people."

Richard had always disliked standing on ceremony. He held

his hand out to Cora. "I leave the morning's entertainment to my lady. Shall we celebrate your wedding by testing our skills in the training yard, bread and cheese be damned?"

What the devil? Why would Cora accompany them to the training yard?

Cora grinned from ear to ear. "How did you know, my lord?"

"Your father, of course. I'm surprised it was not negotiated into your bride price."

Adam did not like being left out of the conversation.

Richard turned to him. "The bow, brother. Your wife is more skilled with the longbow than any man in the Maxwell clan. Was allegedly named champion of that feat two years ago at the Tournament of the North."

Cora stepped forward, her hands on her hips. "Until it was ruled a woman may not be declared victor."

Aye, here was more proof, had he needed any—the demure maid who had walked down the aisle was not his wife. *This* was the woman he had married, and Adam quite enjoyed her.

"I mean to say—" she looked at Adam, "—it is absurd for anyone to think a woman could master the art better than a man."

He nearly laughed. It was a challenge, there was no question of that, and he could not wait to see her shoot.

CHAPTER 7

*J*f it was uncommon for a woman to shoot a crossbow, it was even more so for one to shoot a longbow, considering the back and arm strength that was needed. It was only after much cajoling that Cora's father had allowed her to even try. From the moment she first heard the tale of the Welsh longbow arrow that had killed Edwin, the son of the King of Northumberland, Cora had been determined to master the skill. It had taken her years of practice to reach the target, and even longer to shoot with accuracy and speed, but she had never lacked determination.

Once she'd proven herself, her father had supported her interest in the longbow, arranging for lessons with his cousin, the greatest archer in England, and commissioning a specially designed bow for her. Though her father had initially refused to allow her into the training yard with the lads, she'd worn him down in time, and the entire clan loved to watch her shoot.

After all of her practice, there was none better than she.

At home she had trained every morning and before dusk. Her mother hadn't understood. Her sister had thought she was mad. But to Cora, there was no greater pleasure than forgetting everything in the world save the feel of a bowstring on her cheek, taut, waiting for her command.

"I choose a test of skills," she said now, looking into Adam's eyes.

He held out his hand and stopped her before they left the keep. "Cora, you cannot—"

"Adam," interjected Richard, "allow the woman some space. How will she walk with you hovering so?" With that, he took her arm and escorted her outside. This was working out beautifully. Although it was still early and her stomach grumbled for lack of food, Cora could not be happier. Her husband would be properly appalled and she would be one step closer to her goal without actually embarrassing him in front of Sir Richard.

For some reason, she was hesitant to do so. She knew Richard's approval meant more to Adam than anything. And at first she'd thought to use that fact. But after last night, she felt a tug, a softening, for her husband.

She couldn't look him in the eye, so she was glad Richard had taken her arm. After what happened between her and Adam last eve, Cora wasn't sure she could ever look at him again.

They entered the yard, which was quiet at this hour save for a few soldiers who had either opted not to break their fast or risen early to start their workouts. The armorer, standing in front of the small external armory, gave Cora a curious glance when she asked for her longbow.

"'Tis not yew, my lady?" The bearded man handed her the weapon.

"Nay, ash," she replied. Cora was proud of the weapon, which had been made to match her height. He handed her practice arrows and then pointed her toward the targets at the other end of the training yard.

Anxious to begin, Cora picked up the bow—which was when she realized she already had multiple sets of eyes looking at her.

What had she done? She was used to being watched at home, but somehow this felt different.

There was no time to consider it. She was accustomed to shooting quickly—waiting made her nervous. Thankful for her fur-lined tunic, a cape would have been much too cumbersome, Cora found her mark and took her position across from it.

"My lady," called the armorer, "that target is reserved for—"

She looked back at the man, but Adam waved for her to continue, and the armorer fell silent.

Cora ran through her trainer's instructions. *Do not hesitate. If you find your life in danger, there will be no time to set and contemplate, only shoot.* And she did just that. Her arrow sailed through the early morning air and hit the target in the same spot it planted itself most days. Directly in the center. Where it belonged.

She turned, smiling, and stopped cold. What was the matter with them? Every one stood agape, staring. It was an impressive shot, but not so much so that they should cease their training. She'd hit targets farther than that one.

Richard approached her.

"That was a fine shot, my lady."

He took another arrow and handed it to her. "Show me?"

Cora took a step back. "Pardon, my lord?"

"I've never seen a shot that quick, that accurate, at such a distance."

"Tell her," one of the men shouted.

"How do you test the skills of longbowmen in Scotland?" Richard asked.

"Test?" she asked blankly. "I imagine the same way you do. Accuracy, speed of shots."

"Distance?" Richard asked, his eyes twinkling.

"I suppose," she said.

Richard pointed to where the remainder of the targets were arranged, a considerable distance closer than the one she had hit.

"The one you hit, my lady, is what is known in England as

multum parma. It's a shot reserved for the most experienced archer. The man who consistently hits it becomes the master archer and trains all others."

"Or woman," she corrected.

"As I said, most impressive. Can you show me your trick?"

Richard hurried over to the armory and returned with a bow that was considerably longer than her own. She stood to his left and repositioned him. Placing her gloved hand over his, Cora made another adjustment. It was gratifying to realize he was actually listening to her suggestions.

Richard was a handsome man, she realized. Similar in height to Adam, he exuded the same confidence, perhaps more so as an earl's son. Their mannerisms were also similar. And while Richard's hair was a shade darker, his cheekbones not quite as pronounced, the men had to make quite a sight whenever they traveled together.

He did not, however, make her feel the way Adam did when he was near.

"Will you remember that position?"

"Aye," he responded.

"Good, now drop your hands. When you reposition yourself, do not stop to think. Just bring up the arrow in one swift motion —then shoot."

He looked at her as if she were mad.

"I haven't been on the battlefield myself, but I'm told the enemy gives you little time to get into position and contemplate your shot."

"Very well." He did as she instructed, and though his shot at the long target was respectable, the arrow planted itself quite a distance from the center.

"Well done, my lord." She smiled as Richard bowed to her.

When she turned back to Adam, his expression startled her. She hadn't witnessed his anger before, not for all her needling, but there was no doubt her husband was angry now. He glared at her and Richard as if something were amiss. It was only when Richard chuckled that she realized what was happening.

He was jealous.

Which was just as well since her display of archery had not seemed to put him off. Far from it.

As he continued to glare, albeit with a glint in his eye, Cora's breath caught. She had to remind herself the attentions of her husband were not welcome.

"Shall we continue to practice?" she asked.

Richard laughed again as he looked from her to Adam.

"Indeed, we shall."

Hours later, her stomach indicated it was time to rest. Back home, Cora would often spend an entire day in the training yard, sometimes forgetting to eat.

"I'll leave you to your practice, Sir Richard."

With a wink, he picked up another arrow.

Cora handed her equipment to the armorer and took two steps before a hand grabbed her from behind.

"Oh, Adam. You scared me."

His expression did not reassure her. How long had he been there? He had not joined her and Richard at target practice, and last she'd seen him, he had been the target of a four-man attack in the training yard, fending off sword attacks from so many places she'd thought her heart would stop beating at one point. What was he doing? Was one training partner not enough? He'd get himself killed!

He didn't speak, but he threaded his arm through hers and fairly dragged her toward the keep, leading her along the back and into the gardens in which she'd taken such an interest these past few days. Even with their limited resources, the area was beginning to look less like a kitchen supply and more like a place of refuge and relaxation.

"Get out," Adam barked at the gardener.

The poor man did as he was told, leaving them quite alone,

surrounded by hedges as tall as her husband. Adam pulled her toward him.

"You are mine, Cora."

Oh. That.

He brought his lips to hers so swiftly she didn't have time to think. His tongue demanded a response, and she gave one. His hands rose to cup both of her breasts. He squeezed gently, and she could not hold back a sound from deep within her throat.

She wanted her husband.

It could not be. But it was.

He pulled away abruptly.

"What did you think you were doing?"

She pretended not to understand.

"If you want to look at any man the way you are now, it will be me and only me."

He thought she looked at Richard that way? Was he mad?

"Is that so? And what about you, Adam? You'll look at no other woman now that we are married?"

"Of course I—" He stopped.

"That's what I thought. Pardon me, *my lord.*"

She backed away and ran from the garden into the hall, no longer hungry. She was such a fool. Despite all her intentions, all her plans, he could make her swoon with a mere touch, a mere kiss. Well, no longer. But when she reached the stairs within the keep, Cora was stopped by the very man whom she was not allowed to "look" at.

"Are you all right, my lady?"

She swallowed and tried to rid herself of the intense anger coursing through every part of her body. How could she so easily allow herself to have feelings for an Englishman?

"Aye, my lord," she managed to say in an even tone. "Many thanks for—"

"Come, you haven't eaten all day. Surely you don't plan to skip the meal?"

"I will have something brought up, but I assure you that you will enjoy your meal. Langford's cook is a master."

"I've heard," he answered wryly. "Lady Cora—" Richard looked around the hall, presumably searching for Adam, "—you can speak freely with me. Adam is akin to a brother, I want him…and you…to be happy. He deserves it, and I suspect you do as well."

He seemed so sincere, Cora contemplated telling the man everything. But she could not.

"Thank you for the kind words. But there is naught to concern you."

He cocked his head.

"Truly."

The earl's son did not look convinced.

"I know this is not easy for you, Lady Cora. If I were given no choice but to leave my home and reside in the Scottish Highlands for the remainder of my days…"

He shuddered, and Cora laughed at the look of genuine disgust on his face. As servants hustled around them to make last-minute preparations for the mid-day meal, Cora re-considered her decision to retreat to her chamber.

"But you've married an honorable man. The best one I know. And judging from my father's assessment of your clan's importance in brokering peace along the border, I can understand the need for such a match. But that does not mean adjusting will be easy…or smooth."

Adjusting. Perhaps it could be done. Her father may say otherwise, but aside from him, there was not one member of Clan Maxwell who wouldn't understand her desire to leave England and go back home to Scotland, where she belonged. Where she would be reunited with her sister and her mother. Even her father, no matter how disappointed he'd be in her.

Remembering her goal, Cora tried another tactic.

"Our marriage was successful in keeping the peace, for now. But surely that will not last. It is only one day, after all."

"The Day of Truce? Aye. One day that will lay the foundation for others to follow."

He sounded like her father.

"Adam wants to please you." She wasn't sure what had made her say that, only that it was true—and it was the reason she could not bring herself to follow her original plan.

Richard raised his eyebrows. "I suppose he does."

"I leave you to your meal. Good day, sir."

Cora inclined her head and walked slowly up the stairs.

She needed to be alone.

She needed to go home.

Adam entered the great hall and clenched his fists. His white-hot anger was directed at the most unlikely person. He couldn't remember ever being this upset with Richard.

Moments ago, he'd entered the keep to see Richard and his wife sequestered near the staircase, heads bent together in intimate conversation—something she'd withheld from Adam more often than not these last days. The sound of their murmuring had flitted to him across a room that, thanks to her, now smelled like germander. He rather liked the new smell.

But he most assuredly did not like what he'd witnessed.

"Richard!"

Richard's eyes scanned the crowded hall before landing on him. He raised a hand in greeting, but Adam did not follow suit. Instead, he stalked toward a small storeroom, glancing back only once to ensure that Richard had taken his silent cue to follow.

"What the devil—"

"What the hell do you think you're doing?"

Richard took a step back and stared at him. Then promptly burst into laughter.

"You think—"

"What I think is that my wife seems to find more pleasure in your company..."

He stopped. This was the very topic he'd hoped to avoid discussing with Richard—and he was the one who'd brought it up.

All humor dropped off Richard's face. "What is it, Adam?"

How was he supposed to answer without embarrassing himself? Without disappointing the earl, who did not need any extra worries right now? He should have let the matter drop, but the sight of the two of them together...

"I know you trust me," Richard said.

"Of course I do." Adam ran a hand through his hair. "Jesus."

"Then what is it?"

"Richard, I..." He wasn't sure how he'd planned to end that statement, but he needn't have worried.

"I know about your agreement," Richard said without mirth.

"How?"

"Secrets are not kept in a castle, and servants are less loyal to a new lord." He clapped him on the back. "Adam, you've nothing to worry about. Your wife has not done anything untoward. Nor have I."

Of course not. The struggle of the last week—of staying away from her when he only wanted to be near her—had maddened him. "I'm not sure what came over me."

"'Tis obvious, is it not?"

Adam could only see a portion of Richard's face in the darkened storeroom, but he knew what the man implied.

"I am not in love with my wife. I hardly know her."

Richard remained silent.

"I apologize." The words felt so miniscule, but he had to say something.

"What in the devil do you have to be sorry about?"

"You and your father asked so little of me after I took so much."

"You can't be serious, Adam."

Adam shook his head.

"So that's what your wife was getting at." Richard grabbed his arm. "Listen to me. You are family. Father and I will never forsake you or cast you aside, no matter what."

"I have failed your father."

"Adam," Richard raised his voice, "you're not listening to me. You are one of us. You are a Caiser. It's why you've been given this." He gestured out the door with his hand. "It is your right. Do you understand me?"

Adam looked at Richard's face. Part of him had known these things, but it was different to hear Richard say it aloud. His heart thumped heavily in his chest.

"If Cora Maxwell marched back to Scotland this very moment, you would still be lord of Langford. If you lost the damn castle to the Scottish, you would still be my brother."

Richard released his arm.

Adam didn't know what to say. He was rarely speechless, but he was afraid he'd embarrass himself if he spoke.

"Now, go win that stubborn lass to your side. I've seen you do it with maids you didn't love, so it should be an easy task."

Adam wanted to argue, but he was afraid Richard was right. He'd told himself that what he felt for Cora was simply lust. He'd never been denied by a woman he wanted this much.

But it was more than that. Somehow he'd fallen in love with the woman who was determined to make his life hell. Who was deliberately goading him. Did she really think he'd set her aside?

Never.

He would simply have to redouble his efforts.

"Richard, I need your help."

"Anything, brother. What do you have in mind?"

CHAPTER 8

our days after Richard's arrival, Cora was no closer to
going home. After realizing Adam was jealous, she'd
hoped Sir Richard would unwittingly assist her in her mission,
but her husband simply smiled every time she spoke to the
earl's son.

Each night their routine was the same. And though he came to
their chamber a bit later with Richard in residence, each night he
asked about her day. Their quiet conversations were sometimes
lighthearted, and others more poignant.

He told her of the earl's sickness, and Cora was genuinely sad
for him. It was clear Adam saw the man more as father than overlord. And from what Richard had told her, and from the way he
treated her husband, he truly was a part of their family.

And though she slept in Adam's bed, he had not touched her
since that first night. Surely she was not disappointed. But as she
lay next to him, Cora thought about his touch...the feeling of his
lips on hers. Of his fingers inside her. While she knew she should
be considering more ways to torment him, the memory of his
caresses tormented her instead.

Despite the temptation, Cora was determined not to relent. She would merely direct her thoughts elsewhere.

When Adam had learned of her propensity for the bow, Cora had hoped he would allow her to train with the men. She'd done so back home, and her husband was accommodating in many ways. But on this, he would not budge.

Until today.

This morn, he'd left her a message to meet him in the training yard after she broke her fast. Walking swiftly through the courtyard, Cora waved to a knight she recognized from the evening before. The people of Langford had finally begun to accept her as one of their own. If only she could do the same.

"Welcome, my lady," Richard called out as she made her way through the wooden gate of the training yard.

She could hardly hear him over the clanging of swords. Adam, it seemed, was fond of this place. He'd spent much of his time here in the last few days, leaving administrative duties to the steward.

"I'm told you requested my presence." She addressed her husband, who was dressed casually in hose and a linen shirt that hung loosely around his tanned neck. Her traitorous heart skipped a beat—just as it seemed to do every time she spied the man.

She found herself looking at his eyebrows. They were fuller than most, which gave him a foreboding appearance when he was serious. And he towered over every other man in the yard.

She forced herself to look elsewhere.

"Aye. A word if you please?"

Adam guided her toward the armory. The men around them pretended not to stare, but it was evident they were not accustomed to a woman in the training yard.

"This ends today, Cora."

This?

"I propose a challenge."

"I'm sure I don't understand."

72

His eyes pinned hers, the green specks sparkling in them. "Did you really think I would set you aside? Do you know how rare such a circumstance is in England? Perhaps it's commonplace in Scotland, but when a man weds a woman here, he promises to love and protect her. For all time."

As he spoke, Cora felt the blood draining from her face.

"So you do not deny it?"

She was weary of lying to him. Of working against him, or trying to. "Nay, I do not." She looked him straight in the eyes. "I want to go home."

The hurt in his eyes surprised her. He cared only for the land and title their union had brought him, did he not? But there was no time to mull it over—the fleeting expression was so quickly replaced with a look of anger, Cora was sure she had imagined it.

"You want to go back to Scotland? Go."

Was he serious?

"I challenge you to a contest, wife. One shot. If you are closer to the mark, I will send word to your father that I've appealed for a judicial separation."

Cora's eyes widened. "Why would you do such a thing?"

"I've no wish to spend my days with a wife whose only desire is to leave her husband's side."

"But the agreement? Langford?"

"I will worry about the repercussions. *You* will ensure your father will not retaliate."

She nodded readily. "Aye. I will do so. But you realize, Adam…" She didn't want to voice it aloud lest he change his mind, yet she still found herself saying it, "You will be unable to remarry."

His expression did not change. "I have no need for a wife."

What does he mean by that? Cora wasn't sure she wanted to know.

She took a deep breath. "And if you win, I will remain here, at

Langford." She had already started to walk away, eager to begin. To settle this matter once and for all.

"Nay."

She spun back around.

"Nay?"

"As I said, I'd prefer a willing wife. If you win, you're still free to leave."

She didn't understand. Cora looked around, but no one other than Richard watched their discussion—and he was distant enough not to hear them. Did he know what Adam proposed? Nay, it would kill Adam to admit such a thing to a man he revered.

"If I win, you will give me your virginity. Tonight."

Nay! She could not! "Adam…"

"You know as well as I do that divorce is not possible. Neither of us has been abusive or unfaithful, and I've no desire to have a reputation for either. We will still be married either way. But I give you my word, I will tell no one the marriage was consummated. Provided, of course, a child is not conceived from our union."

"But if you choose to—"

"Cora, look at me."

She did—and immediately wished she had not. The pain in his eyes was now so evident, she felt her own eyes fill with tears. She did not want to hurt him. Cora just wanted to go home, back to where she belonged. If only he…nay, Cora would rather live alone than with the pain of enduring a loveless marriage like her parents. And unlike her mother, she had neither kin nor friends to fill the void.

"Either way, you can leave. On the morrow."

How could she best him with her hands shaking as they were? But he was giving her a way out. And she had no choice but to take it.

"Very well."

At those words, Adam turned from her and spoke with the armorer. He returned a moment later with her bow. She took it from him and walked briskly to the target. Richard stood in front of it as if expecting her. The bow was usually a part of her, but today it felt foreign. Heavier than usual.

"Good day, my lady." Richard inclined his head. He was dressed more formally than Adam, in a dark blue tunic threaded with silver.

"My lord."

Richard handed her one wooden arrow.

"We will be using the 400-yard target, my lady. You will each loose one arrow at a time. The owner of the arrow deemed closest to the target will be declared the winner."

So, he knew about the contest, if not the terms. She nodded, anxious to begin.

"Sir Adam has agreed to allow you first choice."

She glanced back at her husband, who stood so close behind her she could hear his even breathing. He was preparing, and she must do the same.

Cora closed her eyes and imagined the target. When she finally opened her eyes and stepped to the line drawn in the dirt by Sir Richard, she was ready.

Taking aim, Cora did not pause but instead pointed her arrow into the sky and let her shot loose. It sailed high before descending toward the target. She held her breath, realizing for the first time since she'd accepted the bow from Adam that the normally noisy training yard was completely silent.

The English knights knew the rules of this contest even if they did not know the stakes.

"A fine shot, my lady." The gruff voice from behind her sent shivers down her back.

She stepped aside and allowed Adam to replace her position.

It was a good shot on the outermost edge of the center. From this position, it would be nearly impossible to defeat.

Cora smiled until she realized what her shot likely meant.

Richard handed Adam his arrow. Cora watched as he took aim, and for the first time since he had suggested the contest, she began to worry. His position was that of a man who knew the longbow well. She'd heard of her husband's prowess in battle, of his mastery of the lance in tournaments, but she'd never seen him practice with the bow. She'd assumed his skill with the bow was passing fair. But Cora's palms began to sweat as his shot descended and—unbelievably—grazed by her own, landing in the middle of the target. The bow slipped from her hand as the crowd cheered.

She stared in disbelief.

"How..."

Before she could finish, her husband leaned toward her and whispered into her ear.

"I look forward to seeing you later this evening, wife."

And then he strode from the yard without a backward glance. Activity slowly resumed around the yard, but Cora could not process what was happening around her. She could not do anything other than stare at his arrow.

It was an impossible shot.

"He is more skilled than I realized." She said the words aloud to no one in particular.

"You would be surprised, Lady Cora, at your husband's many skills," said Sir Richard. His crooked smile was the only confirmation she needed.

He *did* know.

The knave held out his arm and she took it. What other choice did she have? For, like her husband, Cora was a woman of her word. And though she would not be leaving in the exact manner she'd expected, this was, at least, her last night in England.

Tomorrow she would be going home to her family.

Adam's hand stilled as he prepared to enter his bedchamber.

Thanks to Richard's plan, he had one more chance to convince Cora of how good they could be together. He knew Cora cared for him...desired him. Her eyes betrayed her even if she refused to admit it. And since he disentangled her each morning before she woke, Adam didn't think his wife realized she slept against him each night.

For a moment, he had worried tonight would not happen.

Richard was so skilled with the longbow, he was called on to train men throughout Northumbria. Though her ability was impressive, Adam was sure his friend had only asked for her advice as a kindness, a way of drawing her out by playing to their common interest. Perhaps it's what had first angered him about their camaraderie.

Adam had learned some of Richard's skill by proxy, but the longbow was not his weapon of choice. For the last three days, he had shot arrow after arrow until his hands ached and Richard begged him to stop to take a meal. He'd hardly seen his wayward wife, or anyone, with the exception of the other knights, whose curious looks had finally been mollified today.

Though none but Richard knew why, of course. They only knew he trained with a vengeance and, by some miracle, was victorious.

Damn if his wife hadn't nearly bested him.

She did not attend supper, and he knew from Clare that she had retired hours earlier to their bedchamber.

When he opened the door, darkness greeted him.

He inhaled, the scent of rosewood reminding him, as if he needed a reminder, of who occupied the room. Before Cora arrived at Langford, the castle and its keep had been well fortified but not particularly inviting. The small changes she'd made had begun to show themselves everywhere he turned. And though he was a practical man, Adam could appreciate the effort she'd put into improving a home she did not believe was hers.

He would have to prove otherwise to her.

As was his custom, no servants or attendants remained in the chamber. Its sole occupant sat in front of the fire sipping what he presumed was wine. Their nightly habit of drinking by the fire was one he planned to continue.

First, he had to convince her to stay.

He could see her clearly now. Navigating around a wooden chest, Adam stopped abruptly. Cora's unbound hair flowed down her back and shoulders, but that wasn't what had startled him. She wore the chemise from their wedding night. He remembered the feel of the soft silk and forced himself to breathe.

This night was for his wife. His pleasure would come later.

"Good eve, Cora."

She didn't turn to him but whispered, "Good eve, Adam."

It would be a long night indeed.

His wife began to stand.

"Nay, remain where you are." He poured himself a goblet of wine and sat opposite her, just as he'd done that first night they were together.

"But our arrangement—"

"Can wait."

She finally looked at him, and Adam had to rely on years of training to school his thoughts away from picturing her full lips on his—

"How did you manage that shot?"

The look in her eyes, a mixture of curiosity and affront—she was not used to losing with her bow—tipped his lips into a smile. "Richard," he said simply.

Her brows furrowed.

"I'm passing fair with the bow, but it was Richard's tutelage these past few days that allowed me to win today."

"I see."

Cora's forlorn expression nearly made him change his mind about claiming his reward. "You're disappointed to have lost."

She shrugged. "To have done so with the longbow, aye. Very few have bested me with it."

So she was saddened more by her hurt pride than having to give herself to him. That was encouraging.

"Are you nervous, Cora?"

She didn't appear to be. Bedding virgins was not something he was accustomed to, so this would be new for both of them.

"Nay." She glanced at the canopied bed.

He stood and refilled his cup. Cora inclined her head and he refilled hers as well.

"Will you go home?" He tried to sound casual.

She had the decency to look embarrassed. "Aye. Though my father will be furious."

If she were actually leaving. He could have easily made his reward that she not leave. Had considered it. But Adam wanted her to stay on her own accord.

"But you believe he will allow you to remain in your home."

Her sharp glance was his only answer.

"And what of you? Will the earl be as furious?"

He considered it seriously. Before his discussion with Richard in the storeroom, he would have expected the earl to be disappointed in him, if not furious. Now, he considered all he knew of the man. Of their relationship. Of the many years he'd spent trying to prove his worth to him. And Richard.

Perhaps he'd been wrong.

"I would have thought so, aye. But now I'm unsure."

He understood Cora's confused expression and could hardly reconcile it himself.

"I've been indebted to him my whole life and always thought "son" and "brother" were merely words. But I wonder now if they were not much more."

That Cora listened intently encouraged him.

"It may not be as necessary to prove myself to Spencer," he finished, unable to explain properly.

"It may not ever have been necessary," Cora whispered.

She was right.

But it was too painful to think of the earl now. "You asked about my ability to shoot, but what of yours, my lady?"

His wife's shoulders relaxed. She took a sip of wine and smiled for the first time since he'd entered the bedchamber.

"My father did not approve at first. But I'd heard tales of the Welsh longbow and begged to be trained. Along the border, the Englishman's tactics are our own—"

"And the reverse is true," he allowed.

"Aye. So it was not unknown to the soldiers with whom I trained. One man in particular is responsible for my skill."

"Tell me."

"Alan Maxwell, my father's cousin. He lived in Northumbria for a time. Was married to an Englishwoman."

"Was?"

"She left him."

She said it with such resentment that Adam immediately knew it was partly this English woman who was to blame for his current predicament.

While he waited for her to continue, he tended to the fire, adding a log and allowing the flames to breath.

"Their marriage was an arrangement, not unlike our own, made in a failed attempt at peace with a border family who raided our land mercilessly."

A common occurrence along either side of the border.

"When the small demesne she inherited was attacked and burnt to the ground by English reivers, Alan brought her north, to Scotland. But as he tells it, the woman hated everything about us —always did."

"As he tells it?"

"I was but a babe."

Did she speak so freely because she thought to leave the next day?

"And your cousin?"

She shrugged her shoulders. "He let her go. The woman died less than two years later in a raid."

"I'm surprised her family remained along the border. Many have fled the marches to safer ground."

"*We* have not retreated."

She said it with such pride that Adam was reminded his bride was a border maiden. A woman raised in one of the most dangerous places in England or Scotland. How could he have ever thought her meek?

"Nay, you have not retreated."

And neither would he.

CHAPTER 9

*I*t was time.

Cora tried to remain calm. Appear unaffected. She was anything but.

By the time her husband appeared, she'd worked herself into such a state that even two goblets of wine had not calmed her. Unbelievably, she wasn't sure if it was nerves or anticipation that caused her turmoil.

Cora wanted this. She'd be a fool to deny it.

May God forgive her, she wanted to feel the way she had that other night. It would be a memory of him that she could carry away...

He reached for her hand, brought it to his lips, and kissed each fingertip. His lips moved to her palm, the sleeves of her scandalous chemise shifting upward as he trailed a path toward her wrist.

"Cora." His voice was so deep. Her insides tingled the way they did every time he looked at her with a hint of a smile on his lips.

"What are you doing?" she asked. She was so nervous, she hardly knew what words came out of her mouth.

"I'm kissing your wrist. And before the night is over, I will have kissed every inch of your beautiful body."

"Every—"

"Shhh…"

He stood and pulled her up to join him, wasting no time before he lowered his head and began fulfilling his promise by trailing kisses across her neck and her ear. She could feel his breath as he paused and whispered, "Yes, everywhere."

She held onto his shoulders then, unsure if she could stand otherwise.

His warm lips lowered again to her neck, and she lifted her head to give him better access. She was so focused on the feeling of his lips that she didn't react when he lifted her chemise until the cold crept up her legs.

"What—"

He pulled it up so quickly, she had no other choice than to raise her arms and allow it.

She wore nothing underneath it this night, as her husband had just discovered.

He stared at her, and Cora wanted to grab the garment from his hands and cover herself. But as she watched his face, she felt something else. Something dangerous.

"My God, you are perfect."

Before she had time to be embarrassed once more, he'd dropped the shift into a pool on the floor and resumed his ministrations. But this time his lips moved more freely, without hindrance. His hands rested on her hips as he knelt before her and continued to deliver on his promise. He kissed her everywhere… her arms, her stomach. Cora's hands lay on his shoulders, still covered in a clean linen shirt. She ached to pull it off him the way he'd disrobed her. Memories of those hard muscles in his chest and back had haunted her these many nights.

Suddenly, he stopped. Cora looked down as Adam watched her.

"I said every inch, and I meant it, wife."

What did he—

He kissed her breast, and a moan ripped out of her. Cupping them with both hands, he moved his mouth over her nipple and kissed that, too. But he didn't move on as he'd done everywhere else. He took the tip into his mouth and teased it with his tongue.

She could not stand it a moment longer.

"Your shirt," she managed to croak.

Adam lifted his head for the briefest of moments, long enough to pull the shirt off and toss it to the ground. His lips found her other nipple, but now her hands were touching his bare flesh, too. The muscles of his shoulders tensed beneath her fingers.

Enraptured by the feel of him, the look of his flexing muscles, she had not realized his intent. Ever so gently he kissed her...there!

"Adam, you can't!"

"Everywhere."

He stood and lifted her with one easy movement, carrying her to the bed as if she was a babe.

"But surely not—"

Oh God, that was exactly what he intended. Laying her down on the soft feather mattress, he moved so quickly Cora didn't have time to protest. He knelt beneath her, pulled her legs apart, and actually moved to kiss the most intimate part of her body.

She had to stop him. This could not be...

He didn't kiss her, precisely. Instead, his tongue touched the most sensitive spot and she immediately lifted her buttocks off the bed. Toward him, not away.

Her moan mingled with his own sound of pleasure. The crackling of the distant fire was so clear to her, Cora could imagine they were sitting right next to it. She felt and heard everything. As his tongue explored her, all the muscles in her body tensed as one.

"Relax, my love."

His hot breath against her thigh reminded her of his position.

She opened her eyes and watched as he lowered his head once again. The sight of her powerful husband in such a vulnerable position gave her as much pleasure, as much *excitement*, as the exquisite sensations sent through her by the flicking and prodding of his tongue.

That same feeling, the building of sensation… She grasped the cloth beneath her fingers and attempted to hold on, but it was not possible. The wave of pleasure built until it washed over her.

"Now, Cora."

She exploded, moaning and writhing under him. She opened her eyes again, not even aware she'd shut them, and looked into that piercing gaze that never failed to quicken her heartbeat. She could hear the pounding of it as the wave of pleasure began to ebb.

He'd given her fulfillment, twice, yet taken none of his own.

Unselfish.

"What of you?" she asked.

His low, guttural groan was all the answer she needed.

"Yes." She gave him permission he already had. Cora sensed he had been waiting for it nonetheless.

He stood and tore off every remaining item of clothing until he stood, naked, before her. She dared not look away.

"I…there is no way…"

He was going to kill her.

"Aye, there is." He positioned himself above her, and Cora thought twice about their agreement. The haze of passion lifted and reality took its place.

"Cora, listen to me."

She tried, but the thought of that…

She knew what happened next. Or had some vague notion of what was to happen next. It was not possible.

Adam ran his hands from her outer thighs to her waist. They continued upward until they once again found her breasts.

"Close your eyes."

"Adam, I don't believe—"

"Close your eyes, Cora."

She squeezed them shut. Mayhap if she didn't look...

He laughed, a chuckle that made her think, unaccountably, of the first kiss they had shared. Even then, he'd been exquisitely gentle. He would not hurt her.

His fingers teased the peaks that seemed to harden every time he touched them. And then his hands were gone and the mattress sank under his weight. She startled when his lips found hers.

With her eyes still closed, she opened for him. His kiss was gentle, coaxing. His tongue touched and circled, and the kiss deepened. She sighed and wrapped her hands around his neck, pulling him closer.

Unfortunately, when she did so, she felt that part of him on her stomach. Hard and heavy, it was a reminder of the pain that was to come. Her sister, though equally as inexperienced as Cora in the arts of love, had never been shy about gossiping with the servant girls, and she'd told her the first time would be extremely painful.

But the deepening of his kiss brought her back to the present moment, to *him*. His mouth was so incredibly warm and insistent, and his tongue teased as it swirled around her own. She groaned and lifted herself to him.

And then she felt it. Adam had positioned himself so that the tip of his manhood pressed against her. She was still worried, but her desire for him pulsed more strongly than her fear of the pain. "Please, Adam."

He slipped inside her easily. Slowly and steadily until he stopped and tore his mouth from hers.

His hands held him above her, enough that she could barely feel the hardness of his chest against her own. She wanted more and pulled him toward her.

"I will not take what isn't freely given."

He was inside her, the fullness teasing. Cora wanted to give him the same pleasure she'd found. She wanted to feel the entire length of him inside her.

"Take what is yours," she said breathlessly.

And he did.

Adam thrust inside her and Cora nearly screamed. It felt heavenly for a moment, but then the pain intruded.

He stilled and watched her.

She was naked, lying beneath the man who was her husband. Her innocence, gone. But she wasn't sorry for it—nay, she wanted more. The pain faded, replaced with a feeling that was indescribable. She began to move against him.

It seemed that was the signal he'd been waiting for.

Holding himself on his hands above her, Adam drew in and out. She watched as his expression changed from an almost pained look to something softer. He groaned with pleasure, and the knowledge that she did this to him made her want even more. She met him with each movement until they both panted with exertion.

"Oh God, Cora, you are so damn tight."

She wasn't sure what he meant, but Cora knew it was a good thing. That she could bring him so much pleasure made her feel powerful.

She opened her mouth and he took the invitation. He leaned down and captured her mouth as he continued to move, more quickly now. Circling and thrusting, he mimicked the movements with his mouth. She clawed at his back, desperately trying to hold on. But she could not.

She tore her mouth away to ask. To plead. "Adam..."

"Come on, sweetheart."

Cora pulled him even closer to her. The spasms took her by surprise. They intensified, moving throughout her entire body.

She could hear the deep, guttural sound of a man who had claimed her well and truly. It was a primitive sound. A sensual one. With a final thrust, he collapsed on top of her, and Cora held him tight, not wanting the glorious sensations to end.

Breathing heavily, Cora pulled the coverlet to her neck as Adam finally rolled onto the bed beside her.

He chuckled. "A bit late for modesty."

She supposed he was right. But it felt...odd...to be lying in this state next to a man. Her husband.

"I didn't know what to expect, but that..."

"Was perfect," he finished.

She remained silent.

Adam turned to her, leaning on one elbow so casually it was as if he belonged there next to her. She turned away.

"Why, Cora?" he asked softly.

Somehow, she had known this was coming. And after what had happened between them, she owed him this at least.

"It was my fault. I should have taken a guard." She squeezed her eyes shut. "But it was a fine day, and there had not been a raid or attack for over a year."

Cora turned away. She couldn't look at her husband.

"The English reivers were bold. They knew who I was, knew who my father was."

She felt Adam's hand grasp her own and finally turned to him. His eyes were filled with worry. Not condemnation.

"They did not hurt me. But they would have had my cousin not followed me, worried for my safety."

"My God, Cora. I'm so sorry."

She rushed to continue, not wanting to discuss the vile men any further.

"And my parents. Their marriage was arranged, which of course was not unusual. But, well, you've met my father. He loves his daughters, his clan, his country. The idea of peace after so many years of war. But my mother?"

How could she say such an awful thing aloud? Her father did

not love her mother. And she likely felt the same. It was an arrangement, nothing more.

"That is not unusual, Cora." Adam's voice was hesitant. But he did not deny it.

"Aye, but my mother." She sighed. "She is not like me."

His eyebrows drew together.

"She is timid, quite unlike some of the women of our clan. And now that I am wed, Lily will likely do so as well." She shrugged. "She has no other family."

A loud pounding at the door interrupted them.

"My lord, come quickly," Charles yelled from the other side.

In an instant Adam had leapt from the bed, pulled on his braies, and grabbed his sword.

"Don't move," he instructed.

And then he was gone.

While the steward had done a fair job of maintaining the castle, the small demesne had become a target for unsavory characters in the absence of a lord. Adam had ordered his men to send for him in the event of any crimes in the village, which was why Charles had summoned him after the farmer's cows were stolen.

He'd managed to hunt down those responsible, but it had taken all night—a night he'd hoped to spend showing Cora the pleasures he could bring her. The sun was already rising by the time he rode through the gatehouse, and though he'd sent a message to Cora, telling her he would return as soon as possible, a feeling of unease stole over him.

He froze at the sight that greeted him.

Oh God, Cora.

"Is all well?" Richard asked. He accepted a bag from his squire as he prepared to leave Langford as planned. Or rather, two days after he had originally planned to leave for Kenshire. Adam's impromptu archery lesson had delayed his stay.

But it wasn't the sight of Richard that made his blood run cold. It was the woman standing next to him, her horse ready, her bags apparently packed.

"Going somewhere, my lady?" Adam could not keep the sarcasm from his tone. Furious, he wanted to grab her saddlebags and march them back into the keep. Instead, he watched silently as she made preparations to leave him forever.

"Richard has kindly agreed to escort me to the border, my lord. I'll send word to my father's men from there."

She had the decency to look embarrassed. And while everyone present attempted to appear unconcerned, neither Charles nor Clare accomplished the feat. They both looked positively shocked. Adam couldn't blame them. He'd allowed himself to believe she would stay—that he'd earned her trust, and the emotions he felt for her were not one-sided.

He glared at Richard, who raised his eyebrows. Escort her to the border?

Never.

"My thanks, brother. I trust you to keep the lady safe on her journey?"

Adam wasn't sure if she or Richard appeared more surprised.

"Of course. But why did you not wake me?"

Adam knew Richard would wish to take part in the chase, but Langford was his responsibility, and its people needed to know their new lord was capable of taking swift, decisive action against those who thought to take advantage of the transition.

"There was no need," he said simply.

He walked to Cora, and though it hurt him to play any part in her departure, he helped her onto her mount. The crimson fur-lined cape brushed his fingers, reminding him of the smooth silkiness of her legs.

He'd bedded women before, but last eve had been something

entirely different. Adam had fallen in love with his wife. But he'd also given her his word, and he had no choice other than to allow her to leave.

He leaned down to whisper to her. "Goodbye, Cora. Thank you for the gift of last evening."

After she was safely on her mount, he promptly turned to walk away. Richard followed.

"What shall I do, Adam?"

He stopped and embraced his friend. His brother. "Take her home. And tell your father I'm sorry."

"You aren't serious?"

"If there had not been a raid, perhaps..."

"It matters not! She is your wife. Tell her—"

"I will not have a wife who longs for home. Who mistrusts her husband and her countrymen. If she still wants to leave, perhaps it's for the best."

He didn't really believe the words—and he could tell Richard knew it. But what else was there to say? He had tried to court his wife, and he had failed.

Cora was lost to him.

With a final shake of his head, Richard clasped his arm, nodded, and turned away.

Adam never looked back.

CHAPTER 10

*W*hen they stopped to water the horses, Cora recognized the lake from her journey south. She had not spoken to Sir Richard or his men since their departure from the keep. She could tell all of them but Richard were confused, but Cora didn't care.

She wasn't sure if she'd care about anything ever again.

She had gotten exactly what she'd thought she wanted. She should be elated. Excited to see her family, her sister. To hear the familiar sounds of her clansmen and Alan's soft-spoken words of encouragement as they trained in the yard.

Instead, every limb in her body felt heavy. Her chest ached, likely for the broken heart she'd left behind. Somehow, unbelievably, she'd done the one thing she had sworn she would never, ever do.

Fall in love with an Englishman.

But it mattered not. When she spoke of her parents' loveless marriage, he agreed it was typical. At least back home, she would be surrounded by a family and clan that loved her.

But the thought of Adam doing what he'd done to her the night before…

"Are you ready, my lady?"

Sir Richard had been a polite, if silent, escort.

"Aye." She stood and followed him toward their mounts.

The sun, high in the sky now, warmed her enough for Cora to take off her cloak. Underneath, the plain, serviceable day gown matched her mood.

"Sir Richard, I meant to ask. My father will surely question me...what happened to the man who saved you that day?"

That day. The Day of Truce. The day responsible for her current predicament.

Richard spoke to one of the men who rode ahead, presumably ordering him to scout, then turned back to her.

"Sir Hugh Waryn, you mean," he replied. "I count him a dear friend."

"I'm glad for it. Having friends along the border is better than counting your enemies," Cora said.

"That sounds like something Adam would say," Richard replied, quirking his mouth into a grin.

The sound of his name drew a sharp pain in her chest.

But he was right. "He does speak of peace often. And also talks highly of you," Cora said.

Richard looked as if he considered his next words carefully. Cora wished he hadn't brought up the subject of her husband.

"And he of you."

That was all he said. What had she hoped for? Professions of Adam's undying love for her? Assurances that their marriage would not lack for love? What did it matter?

It matters a great deal.

Last eve, Adam had told her 'I am not your father.' But words were hollow, were they not?

She froze.

"What is it, my lady?"

"My lord, may I have a word?" One of Richard's retainers called to him.

"Pardon, my lady."

Cora stuck her hand in the folds of her traveling gown and squeezed the sealed letter. Her heart began to beat furiously as she lifted it, tore the seal, and began to read.

As suspected, it was the monk's handwriting. He'd taught her to read and write, but her mother could not do so. Her hands began to shake as she continued to read.

"Your marriage is a noble act, my daughter, but one you should not regret. May you find the love with your husband that I did not. Your father is a good man and loves you dearly. As do I. Have courage and all will be as it should."

"Lady Cora, are you well? You look quite pale."

If she was pale, there was good reason for it.

"I may have made a mistake."

He looked at her as if she were mad.

"My lord, you know Adam well." She wasn't sure how to proceed.

"If you're asking if Adam loves you, that's an easy question to answer. I know the man better than I do myself and have never seen him like this, if you'll pardon my saying so. I could tell immediately he was besotted by you."

As if he'd said too much, Richard abruptly turned away.

Cora stopped him.

"I must go back."

He spun toward her, his eyes wide.

"Pardon?"

"Sir Richard. I have made a mistake. A terrible mistake. It will be a wonder if Adam forgives me for what I've done this day. But I must go back. Immediately."

Her heart hammered in her chest. Adam kept his promise to let her go. Risked the anger of his liege and her father, not to mention embarrassment to his people for his wayward wife's actions.

He'd done it because he was an honorable man. One that was

capable of both leadership and love. A different man than her father.

She looked up at Richard, frantic now.

"I beg you, please, take me—"

He had already moved to assist her onto her horse. "To Langford."

To the south. Away from her home. Away from Scotland.

To the man she loved.

Adam was pacing in the solar, waiting for word from Charles, when the door opened. He prepared to set the steward down for taking so long.

But it was not Charles who stood in the threshold.

"Cora?"

She looked as if she'd been riding all day, without pause. Her hair was pulled back in a braid, but wayward strands peeked out from more than one spot. Her gown was dirty and she breathed heavily as if she'd run the entire way back.

She'd never been more beautiful to him.

"Adam—" she rushed into the room and threw herself into his arms, "—I was a fool."

He held his wife so tightly that he feared he'd crush her. He didn't want to let go. He never wanted to let go.

"Our vows…you said …it was a stupid thing to do. You're right —you aren't my father. And these people. They're kind and giving, like you. It makes no difference that they're English. And I do trust you." Her words tumbled out so fast, Adam had a difficult time understanding what she said.

"And the contest. You kept your word. I'm so sorry." Adam felt the wetness of her cheeks on his shoulder.

"Shhh, my love. Don't think me too noble." He kissed her face, her lips. She opened for him immediately and Adam pressed himself against her. She was back.

Her mouth felt soft and smooth beneath his own. Adam wanted to tear the gown off her body and show her just how much he wanted her. Needed her. But he had to tell her first.

"I love you, Cora."

Her lips turned up in the most beautiful smile he'd ever seen. God, she was magnificent.

"And I love you. I didn't want to leave. I—"

He placed a finger on her lips. "It matters not. You're here, where you belong."

"Aye. With you." She looked up at him quizzically. "What did you mean when you said 'Don't think me too honorable?'"

He smiled wryly. "Just that I didn't plan to keep my word for long." He pointed to a packed bag near his chair.

"You were coming for me!"

"Of course. Do you honestly believe I'd let the woman I love escape back to the wilds of Scotland? Where everyone knows all manners of hideous beasts roam?"

She laughed. A delicate, delicious sound.

"I've heard they are quite terrifying, those Scots."

"Especially the ones at the border. 'Tis said the women train with the men, if you can imagine such a thing."

He kissed her again, allowing his hands to roam toward her ample bosom.

His voice lowered. "'Tis said their maids are insatiable, that it takes a lifetime to satisfy their lust."

"That, my English lord, is something I intend to find out."

Adam looked forward to such a discovery.

THE THIEF'S COUNTESS EXCERPT

"*T*hieving bastards." Sir Geoffrey Waryn wasn't talking to anyone in particular, but his uncle wouldn't let the comment pass.

"Should I remind you this raid was your idea?" Sir Hugh Waryn shouted, riding next to him. "Besides, neither of us should comment on thievery."

Ignoring that last remark, Geoffrey urged his horse to a gallop. He needed to undo what he'd done, and that meant finding the others before the daylight faded. They couldn't be far ahead, but the forest was dense enough to restrict his view.

"There," he whispered. The trees had opened to a small clearing, and there they were, the small gang of reivers Geoffrey and his uncle had aligned themselves with a few weeks earlier. The crisp autumn air filled his lungs as he deliberately slowed his breathing, preparing for the worst.

He should have trusted his instincts and his uncle's counsel. Even among thieves, these men had no honor. The raid had gone well until the lord's young son had made an appearance. Then, before Geoffrey realized what Elliot and his cousins were planning, they'd sped away with the boy in tow.

Stealing cattle was one thing. Geoffrey and his uncle needed resources, badly. Stealing a lad was quite another.

The last thing he wanted was a fight with these men, but he would not let them kidnap the boy.

Geoffrey easily passed all four mounted reivers, including the one who held the young boy, and angled his horse in front of the front rider. His uncle skirted a massive oak to remain at his side.

"Give him up, Elliot," Geoffrey shouted to the startled man in the lead.

The leader abruptly stopped, leapt from his horse, and grabbed the lance at his side.

Damn. Elliot isn't going to make this easy. Well, neither will I.

A leering grin spread across his former ally's face. "If you want him, take him."

Swinging his own lance into place, Geoffrey decided to make a quick demonstration of the leader as the other men began to dismount from every side. Towering above his opponent, Geoffrey swung his lance, laying the man flat on the ground with two deft strokes. He tossed the lance aside, slipped his dirk from its leather sheath, and held the knife to Elliot's neck. The leader's eyes darted to the other riders, one of whom had dragged the bound and gagged hostage with him toward the fight.

"Don't be stupid. You know exactly how this will end." He had no desire to spill the blood of a fellow Englishman.

But he would.

"Drop your weapons." His tone made it clear that it was not a request.

Geoffrey had a bit of a reputation with his lance, and he wasn't surprised when they tossed their weapons to the ground. "I have no desire to call the Elliot family an enemy, but you go too far."

"Sir Geoffrey." Elliot's eyes darted desperately from him to the hostage. "Think of the ransom."

Geoffrey sheathed his dirk and walked swiftly over to the

child. He said nothing as he pulled the boy out of his kidnapper's grasp and lifted him onto his own destrier.

Only then did he turn back to his opponent, who was rubbing his back and attempting to stand. "Elliot, think of your honor."

A ransom that would feed them for months wasn't worth terrifying an innocent young lad. The captive was no more than ten and one, and his eyes were wide and full of tears. Geoffrey's stomach roiled.

Had it really come to this?

"Thank you, milord."

Geoffrey didn't correct him.

"I'm sorry you were so mishandled, boy." After a short ride, he and Hugh dropped the boy off a safe distance from the search party that had been sent out for him.

Without speaking, Geoffrey followed his uncle's lead as they rode away from the sight of the botched raid. Their mounts expertly navigated increasingly uneven terrain as they headed south into the Cheviot Hills. A steep incline and rocky descent finally gave way to a narrow valley surrounded by mountains on both sides. When they reached flat ground, they exchanged a nod, then dismounted to give their horses a much needed rest.

And resumed the argument that had begun before that evening's doomed attempt to steal a few heads of cattle to feed his siblings and sell to retain mercenaries for their campaign.

"I won't do it." Hugh was the last person Geoffrey wanted to contradict, but the stakes were too high. They'd been building momentum, gathering promises from men to fight along with resources, and this wasn't the time to stop. Five years earlier, Scottish raiders had stolen Geoffrey's home, his inheritance. Everything he and his family owned. And he would not rest until his parents were avenged. "I'm not a nursemaid to be ordered about by Caiser's steward."

When his uncle had received word the day before that his assistance was required at Kenshire Castle, the seat of the Earldom of Kenshire, Hugh had shocked Geoffrey by instantly agreeing to the request. He immediately sent word to Geoffrey's siblings that their return would be delayed.

"What of Lettie and Simon? They need the spoils of this raid."

His mother's aunt and her husband cared for Geoffrey's brothers and sister. They took them in when Bristol was lost, but the small manor could hardly sustain itself even without extra mouths to feed.

"Taken care of. The messenger has been properly compensated to deliver the coin we've earned."

Kneeling beside the stream that crisscrossed the valley, Geoffrey cupped his hands against the current. It would be hours before they next stopped to rest.

When he stood, he turned his eyes to the sky, praying for patience, before he finally met and matched his uncle's stare. He couldn't imagine any mission more important than the one they'd spent the last five years preparing for. This was a distraction they didn't need.

"It's no concern of ours if the lady—"

"Sara," said Hugh.

"Fine, Lady Sara. It's not our—"

Once again his uncle cut him off.

"Actually, it is our concern. As I've said before, Lord Kenshire was a friend." Hugh broke eye contact and turned away, his normally proud shoulders slumping slightly as he spoke. The earl had apparently died after a long illness three weeks earlier, and the man's steward had immediately sent for Hugh. It had taken some time for Kenshire's men to find them, but now that the message had been received, his uncle could not be swayed from his decision to attend to the new countess and help her secure her claim.

"When we were young knights, Lady Sara's father and I met at the very first Day of Truce. In truth, I saved his life. Before he was addressed as 'Your Grace,' —" Geoffrey's uncle turned to him again, his stance daring another interruption, "—we were as close as brothers. Later, our paths took us to separate places. I will help his family now."

Geoffrey tossed the stone he was holding. Just like that, his protests no longer mattered. "But what of the men we've gathered? Nothing—" he stressed the word with as much force as he dared, "—is more important than taking back Bristol." They'd spent years gaining support and promises of aid when it was needed. But rather than build on the momentum they had gathered, his uncle would have him head south, away from Bristol.

"I know you're impatient," Hugh said, "but Lady Sara's claim is tenuous. Sir Randolf Fitzwarren believes his claim to Kenshire is strong, and he may have the support he needs to bring an army to Kenshire."

"Fitzwarren? That traitor is Caiser's relative?"

"A distant relation, yes. And desperate for power." Hugh narrowed his eyes. "Lady Sara needs us. I made a promise to her father, and I intend to keep it."

"I'm surprised the earl recognized a man who fought against the king."

"He didn't."

And now he tried to claim Kenshire in the earl's absence. Geoffrey had heard enough. "Then it seems we have no choice. Someday I'll have the full story." He grabbed his horse's saddle to prepare for a ride into the devil's lair. "For now we leave on your command."

He saw his uncle's smirk out of the corner of his eye. What did he have to smile about? Hugh must know their actions would likely be detrimental to them both.

"You win, Uncle," he said, grudgingly resigned to their task. "Let's go start a war."

Lady Sara Caiser was running out of ways to avoid her staff.

She had skipped the morning meal as well as her daily meeting with castle officials, opting for a short ride to the village instead. Discussing castle accounts wasn't her favorite part of the day, but it was still preferable to answering questions about their "guests." Today she'd managed to avoid both thus far. Her good cheer must have shown, because when she walked into the spacious kitchen, Cook said, "It's good to see milady smilin' again."

A flurry of activity greeted Sara. The kitchen staff was scurrying all about, large black cauldrons hung over an open fire and the smell of roasting venison made her mouth water. She reached for a loaf of bread, expecting to get her hand slapped. She wasn't disappointed.

"Breakin' apart a fine loaf before it's cut. Hmph." Cook wiped her hands on her well-worn apron.

Winking at a nearby kitchen maid, Sara reached for the bread again. Making herself sound as pitiful as possible, she said, "I missed breakfast." She tore off the prize and popped it into her mouth.

"Mayhap you should eat with the rest of the household then," the woman replied.

"Perhaps. But how would I avoid Peter then?" She flashed Cook her biggest smile and averted a lecture by making a hasty retreat.

Sara left the kitchen and made her way to Kenshire Castle's main keep. Every step felt heavier than the one before as she approached the ancient stone walls marking the entrance of her home. There was no use in trying to hide from the inevitable.

Lifting her blasted skirts so she could climb the stairs, she made her way to the very place she'd been avoiding. The room attached to the lord's chamber was where her father conducted business. Usually it was a spot that lent comfort to her, but not today.

The only person currently occupying Sara's solar didn't waste any time with pleasantries. Her anxious lady's maid began talking as soon as she opened the heavy oak door. "Our guests are expected tonight, milady."

"Tonight?" If her unusually sharp tone startled Faye, her maid didn't react. The middle-aged woman served as a surrogate mother, friend and, at times like these, a much-needed calming influence. She was well-accustomed to Sara's moods.

Faye guided her to a cushioned stool and began brushing the unruly hair the young countess had inherited from her mother.

"I don't care how renowned these men's 'skills' are. I simply refuse." A knock at the door meant she would quickly be outnumbered. Faye stopped her ministrations to allow the entrance of Sara's steward.

"Lady Sara." Peter made his way toward through the solar. "The kitchen has been informed of the altered supper plans. The guests' rooms are being readied as well."

Of course he'd already seen to the preparations. Peter was stocky for his advanced age, and his full grey beard, gruff manner, and proper dress intimidated those who didn't know him. To Sara, he was like the grandfather she'd never had.

Peter seemed to be gauging her response.

She took a deep breath, determined to remain calm. "About our guests," she started, not wanting to take out her displeasure on a man who was only following orders. Her father's orders, no less. "I'd like to speak to you about them."

"Lady Sara, we discussed this. At length. There is no other option."

As they stared at each other, Peter's bushy eyebrows rose.

She'd seen that familiar look more often since her father passed away. Sara would not doubt herself this time.

"Peter, we don't need those men. They're reivers. Lawless thugs who murder and steal for sport and take advantage of the uncertainty at the border. The thought of being protected by them is … unacceptable." Once, an English marshal whose manor lay just across the border from Scotland had stopped to seek shelter at Kenshire. Sara still remembered his stories of brutal Scottish and English reivers who cared not for the origins of their victims. Master horsemen despite the mountainous terrain, they spent their days rustling livestock, stealing household goods, and even taking prisoners for ransom. She shuddered at the memory, bringing herself back to the present.

But when she looked to Faye for support, her lady's maid tilted her head to the side, which could only mean one thing. "Lady Sara, you know as well as I do that Sir Randolf will not stop until he has his hands on Kenshire."

"But he has no claim!" It infuriated her that a distant cousin could think the earldom was his for the taking simply because she was a woman. Her father had trained her from early childhood to take care of the earldom. He'd left her in charge many times, and she'd proven herself a competent leader before.

So why did he doubt me in the end? Why send for those men? Why betroth me to the Earl of Archbald?

She tried to push the thoughts from her mind.

"Through misadventures, numerous rejected marriage proposals … my lord gave you more freedom than proper," scolded Faye.

Peter and Faye were only trying to help, but that didn't mean she had to agree with how they were trying. Her head hurt from trying to imagine ways she might stop the reivers' arrival. And her impending marriage of convenience, for that matter.

"My lady." Faye resumed her ministrations with the brush.

"We've been through this before. I have no authority to give you orders save appealing to you to consider your father's wishes. But murderers for sport? I hardly think the late Lord Kenshire would have had dealings with such men."

"And if I may," continued Peter, "marriage to Lord Lyonsford isn't a fate worse than death as you'd have us believe."

"Not unless one has no desire to marry an elderly gentleman." She couldn't keep the mockery out of her voice. "His 'vast lands' and 'favored countenance' aside." It was an old argument, but not one that had been settled to anyone's satisfaction.

Neither Peter nor Faye replied. Sara gathered her freshly brushed hair to one side, giving Faye a tight smile of thanks.

"My lady," Peter sighed, "please don't look at us that way. At your age, as an earl's daughter, 'tis a wonder you've not been wed three times over."

Faye nodded. "Lady Sara, earl's daughters simply don't marry for love. But that doesn't mean you won't share affections with Lord Lyonsford."

"And as for our visitors," Peter added, "you must remain Countess of Kenshire until your wedding day."

What was the point of arguing? Everyone in the room knew how it would end. She would be married to the Earl of Archbald, and these border thieves her father had summoned would come to protect her in the meantime.

She was in charge of an entire household—a village!—but not herself.

Sara closed her eyes, not wanting to look at their expectant faces. She was the Countess of Kenshire, but Faye and Peter had a talent for making her feel like a wayward child. Her father would never have let anyone sway him from his decisions.

But he was the one who had wished for both of these things— the engagement and the reivers—and now he was gone.

She stood, smoothing the front of her deep green overcoat,

picking imaginary stray threads off its silver lining. "When do they arrive?"

Both Peter and Faye looked more than a little relieved.

"Anytime now, my lady," Peter beamed.

"Then thank you for preparing the kitchen. Let's be about our day."

She made a quick decision as she watched Peter and Faye exit the room. Sara made her way through the door that adjoined the bedchamber. From the ornate trunk in the corner, which had belonged to her mother, she selected a soft white cloak with a fur-lined collar.

Wrapped up in the cloak, she crept quietly to the great hall and then exited through a side door adjacent to the hall. Though she felt a tad guilty about escaping preparations for the second time that day, she knew her advisors would ensure all was ready for her unwanted guests.

The cloak protected Sara from the crisp air that always accompanied the change in seasons. She was grateful for it as she made her way down a path known only to a few. The "sea path," her father had called it. A gateway to the North Sea.

Eventually she found herself walking through tall grass, her feet sinking deeper into the gritty sand with each step.

How did he do it?

When he was alive, her father had been both reticent and giving, uncompromising and yielding. Somehow he'd demanded respect without asking for it, and he'd always made the right decision. Or so it had seemed.

How?

She straightened her back, resisting the tingle in her cheeks. She would not cry. Her duty was to the hard-working people who lived and worked on the unforgiving coast of Northern England. They needed her to do everything in her power to retain her title. There were so many dangers for her in Northumbria—at least until she had a husband. The border. The Scots. Sir Randolf

Fitzwarren, that vile usurper who tried to steal Kenshire from under her.

For her people, she'd accept Lord Lyonsford. For them, she'd allow the reivers to stay at the keep.

But that didn't mean she had to like it.

The Thief's Countess is **available now** on Amazon.

ALSO BY CECELIA MECCA

The Ward's Bride: Prequel Novella

English knight Sir Adam Dayne, to keep peace along the border, must accept a betrothal to the Scottish Marcher warden's beautiful daughter. Lady Cora Maxwell hates everything English. When Adam proposes a unique challenge, Cora is forced to face her greatest fears and the burgeoning desire he has awakened.

The Lord's Captive: Book 2

After reclaiming his brother's inheritance, Sir Bryce is faced with an unwanted distraction—the sister of his greatest enemy. Divided loyalties pull the English knight and his Scottish captive, Lady Cora, apart even as passion ignites between the unlikely pair.

The Chief's Maiden: Book 3

The Scottish king gives Toren Kerr a dangerous but important mission—kill the English Warden. But when he travels to England to participate in the Tournament of the North, he's immediately drawn to Lady Juliette Hallington. The English noblewoman longs to escape her sheltered life, but learns the very thing she wants most might consume everything she holds dear.

BECOME AN INSIDER

The absolute best part of writing is building a relationship with readers. The CM Insider is filled with new release information including exclusive cover reveals and giveaways. Insiders also receive 'Border Bonuses' with behind the scenes chapter upgrades, extended previews of all Border Series books and a copy of *Historical Heartbeats: A Collection of Historical Romance Excerpts* from various authors.

CeceliaMecca.com/Insider

ABOUT THE AUTHOR

Cecelia Mecca is the author of medieval romance, including the Border Series, and sometimes wishes she could be transported back in time to the days of knights and castles. Although her actual home is in Northeast Pennsylvania where she lives with her husband and two children, her online home can be found at CeceliaMecca.com. She would love to hear from you.

Stay in touch:

info@ceceliamecca.com